DRAGON'S ISOLATION

RED PLANET DRAGONS OF TAJSS #19

MIRANDA MARTIN

CONTENTS

FOREWORD

Don't miss the beginning. It begins with Dragon's Baby and carries on from there!

This work of fiction was inspired by and drawn from the unprecedented experiences we are all going through at the time I write this.

There have been so many acts of bravery, silent warriors, who too often go unacknowledged putting themselves at risk during the time of this pandemic.

I would like to dedicate this book to all of you who have survived. I hope, in some small way, the theme of this story helps you.

We survive and we love. Love is our greatest power and ability. I hope you and yours are doing well and please, splurge on your love for anyone and anything. The world needs all the love it can get.

xoxo,
Miranda Martin

AMARA

I have this theory. Life is nothing but a series of moments. Memories. Each one, good or bad, precious experiences, frozen in time, and filed away. They form who we are and what we will be. Our memories shape us, and the game of life is all about making each moment you have a good one, or at least the best you can make it.

The old me, from before the crash, would never recognize the me today.

"Stop, Daddy!" Malcolm screams, laughing.

He struggles to get away from Shidan, who is holding him tight and blowing raspberries on Malcolm's neck. Malcolm may be screaming, but he's also laughing so hard his face is turning colors. Watching my boys play is one of those good moments.

I've changed. A lot. On the ship, I never wanted kids. I didn't want to settle down or be married or any of this. I also thought I was happy, but then I was always good at lying to myself. I think it's a human trait. We tell ourselves we're happy when we don't know what real happiness is. It's 'normal,' so that must be being happy.

Malcolm squirms out of Shidan's grip, flapping his wings rapidly and getting some space between them before he drops to the floor. He runs behind the makeshift couch I'm sitting on.

"Help me, Mommy!" Malcolm says, giggling.

"You're on your own," I say, trying not to laugh.

"There is no escape!" Shidan roars, laughing and pretending to be a monster, holding his hands out and wriggling his fingers.

He stalks Malcolm with exaggerated motions as they continue playing. It's an effort, but I keep my thoughts focused on this moment. All the stress and worries outside our door are exactly that, out there. Right here, right now—it's us. My family. My loves.

Shidan darts the wrong way, leaving an opening for Malcolm, who zips out from behind the couch and runs for his room. Shidan grabs him as he passes by and throws him up into the air.

"Shidan!" I yell, heart leaping into my throat.

He catches Malcolm, who doesn't stop giggling. "More!"

"He's fine, my treasure," Shidan says, tossing the boy up again.

Every time he does this, my heart stops, my chest constricts, and I'm sure he's going to miss catching him. Is it trust or instinct? I don't know, but I really hate this game. It's too rough.

"Stop," I demand. "You know I hate it when you do that."

He catches Malcolm in midair and tucks him under his arm.

"Of course, my love," Shidan says.

"Ah, Mom," Malcolm whines.

"Ah, nothing," I say. "You're going to give Mommy a heart attack."

"Why would your heart attack you?" Malcolm asks, frowning.

"It's a saying that means your heart stops working," I explain.

"Why would it stop working?" Malcolm asks.

"Because some little boy and his daddy made it so scared that it couldn't keep going," I say, shaking my head.

"Your heart needs to be tougher," Malcolm says. "I'm fine."

"Yes, you are, my love, yes you are," I agree.

My heart swells and tears form in the corners of my eyes as an emotion overtakes me. It's more than my body can hold. Damn it, I hate these moments. They're too big. Too much to contain. The kind of moment I want to lock away and have forever.

"Ah, my love," Shidan says, kneeling in front of me and pulling me into his arms.

He wraps me up in him, the sweet musky smell of him engulfing me, and I sigh. He runs his fingers through my hair, giving me, for a moment, all of his attention. It doesn't last long before Malcolm is wriggling his way between us.

"Group hug!" he says.

"Big hugs!" Shidan squashes our son between us. "Too much love."

"Ahhhh!" Malcolm cries out, laughing.

I let go of Shidan and lean back on the couch. "You're both impossible."

Shidan smiles and shakes his head, moving to sit next to me. He places an arm around my shoulders. Malcolm drops to the floor and grabs some of his toys, or what passes for toys here on Tajss. On the ship I'd have never considered these makeshift things toys for a kid. On the ship, we still had the mass retail mentality though. Here, handmade is everything. Malcolm's action figures are carved pieces of rock that Shidan carefully created for him.

"My treasure," Shidan says, nibbling my ear while he runs the tip of his tail up and down my thigh.

3

I squirm as his warm breath tickles my neck. As I try to move away from him, he throws a leg across my lap and presses his body against mine.

"Little eyes," I murmur, pushing down the excitement rising in my core.

Years. It's been years, and still he turns me on. He pulls his leg off of mine, but not before I'm acutely aware of his arousal digging into my side.

"Right," he says, looking over at our son.

He turns and sits properly. One arm over my shoulders, his tail playing with my hair, we watch Malcolm play. These moments are rare for us, and I treasure them. It's not often we have quiet time as a family. Survival on Tajss is far from guaranteed or easy. Every day is a fight.

"Are you hunting today?" I ask.

"No," he says. "We have a delivery of feed coming today. It's for the bivo herd we're working to domesticate."

"Oh, do you have to go?" I ask, butterflies dancing in my stomach.

I know the answer he's going to give, but it's not going to be the one I want.

"Yes," he says. "It's my duty."

I knew it, of course, but it doesn't change my hope to keep him home. Four days ago, the City was put on lockdown. Ladon, one of the Zmaj warriors, was exposed to something out in the desert. When he got back, he got sick, then fell into a coma. He still hasn't woken up. Ormarr, a Zmaj healer, came to help and now he's sick too.

As soon as Ormarr got sick, that was when Rosalind, our human leader, ordered the City into lockdown. Until we know how this sickness spreads, our only hope is to contain it. We need the Zmaj if we're going to survive this planet—and I need my man.

"They can drop it off and leave it," I say. "They don't even know we're in lockdown yet. Let someone else deal with it."

"The bivo aren't faring well in captivity. They need daily attention," he stops talking and a thoughtful look is on his face. "You know this, my treasure. What is it really?"

"Can't you stay home?" I ask.

I look at him with half-lidded eyes and pouting my lips, making it clear that I'm asking about a whole lot more than if he's going to be home. He doesn't miss the cue because he's always attentive. Which I love.

"Is this an offer?"

"It could be," I say. "If someone goes to bed on time."

"Then I will most definitely be home."

"But you won't stay?" I ask, pushing.

He's bound by honor and duty. It's a trait I love, most of the time, but now it's going directly against what I want, for him to stay home. To be safe.

"It will be fine," he says, turning to our son playing on the floor. "Malcolm, would you like to go with Daddy today?"

Malcolm leaps to his feet, eyes wide and squealing with excitement. "Can I?"

"If your mother is okay with it," Shidan says.

I stare wide-eyed at Shidan while my heart climbs into my throat and cold ice forms in my stomach. I can't believe he's put me on the spot like this.

"I don't think it's a good idea," I whisper.

"Aw, mom," Malcolm whines.

"He'll be fine," Shidan says.

I shake my head mutely. I can't get words past the lump in my throat. A surge of anger forms behind the fear. He's putting our son at risk, and I can't believe it. How is he not taking this seriously?

"You'll be good?" I ask.

"Yes!"

"You won't wander off again?" I ask.

"No!"

"You'll listen to your daddy?" I ask.

"Ugh," Malcolm exclaims, throwing his hands up. "Too many rules! I'll be good, I promise."

"I don't like it," I say.

"So I can go!"

Shidan's smile is broad as he nods enthusiastically, encouraging our son. I don't want to be the bad guy here, and he's backed me into a corner.

"You'll stay away from others and keep Malcolm away from anyone and everyone?" I ask Shidan.

"As much as possible," he says.

"No, period," I insist. "Addison says we need to stay six feet apart at a minimum. You'll keep him that far apart and yourself?"

"Of course, my love," he says.

Malcolm is bouncing from foot to foot, flapping his wings in excitement.

"I'm going out, out-out-out, I'm going out-side!" he sings.

I can't break his heart, and it would be good for him to get some space. He's been cooped up for days now, and his energy is way too much for that. He's been bouncing off the walls.

"All right," I say, my stomach clenching tight. "Let me talk to your father some more first."

"Ah, come on Mommy! Let me go!" He leaps from the floor into my lap.

I bite my tongue as he slams into me, and tears well in my eyes. I suppress crying out my pain as stars fill my vision. I don't want him to feel bad, but *damn*, that hurt.

"Please, Mommy, please, please, please!"

He peppers my face with kisses between each please. It's adorable and helps me ignore the throbbing pain of my tongue.

"Okay, okay," I say. "Go play in your room now."

"Isn't it time to go?" he asks.

"Let me talk to your mother first," Shidan says.

"Okay, don't leave me," Malcolm says, running for his room. There's a massive crash almost the moment he walks in. "I'm fine!"

"What was it?" I call back.

"I'll fix it," he yells.

"You know it's bad, right?" I ask Shidan.

He slides closer to me on the couch and pushes some hair out of my eyes. "I'll help him fix whatever it was," he says.

I nod and agree because I don't want to lose this chance to talk to him without Malcolm in the room.

"Why did you bring that up in front of him?" I ask.

It's clear he's surprised or confused by the look on his face.

"What do you mean, my treasure?"

"You asked, in front of him, about taking him out. You're making me look like the bad guy!"

"Oh," he says, he pulls me close, enclosing me with his body. He kisses down my neck.

"I'm serious," I say, pulling away. "That was not cool."

He rises on his elbow, giving me his full attention.

"I am sorry," he says. "I didn't think it was a big thing."

Are you sure about taking him out?" I ask.

"Of course, why wouldn't I be?" Shidan asks, running his fingers through my hair.

"We're under quarantine," I say. "I don't want you going out, much less him."

"It will be fine," he says, paying more attention to his fingers running through my hair than to me.

"Shidan," I say sternly. "I'm serious."

He stops fiddling with my hair and gives me his full attention.

"Yes," he says.

"Yes, what?" I ask, exasperated.

"Yes, I am sure. Yes, I think it's a good idea. I will not cower in fear. My work must be done, or we will not have food. Already we have shortages. Our stocks are dangerously low, we might have enough food for a week if everyone complies with the rationing."

"That's a big if," I observe.

"Exactly," he says. "The bivo breeding project is our hope for the future. The Tribe's garden is growing well, but it's not nearly big enough to feed the City and the Tribe by itself. Besides, we need meat in our diet."

"I know," I shake my head. "I wish I didn't. I wish I was like all the regular people living out their lives here in the City. They have no idea how close to disaster we dance every day. If they did, they wouldn't have enough worry left over for their bitching about Rosalind."

"That seems to be a human trait," he says.

"Hey, I'm human!" I say.

"No." He shakes his head. "You are an angel sent to me from the stars."

My cheeks warm. "You're cheesy as hell."

"Perhaps, but I am also right." He smiles.

I roll my eyes, but his cheesiness always makes me smile, and it eases my fears.

"Fine," I say. "But that doesn't change the facts. Ladon and Ormarr have the virus. We don't know who else has it. Any human you meet could carry it and we apparently don't get sick. We don't know if the kids can catch it or not. I don't want to risk it. I can't lose you or him."

"My love," he says, shaking his head. "I do not want to argue with you, but I must do what I must. If you prefer, I will leave Malcolm home, but I think it would be good for him to get some sun and air."

"I'm not only worried about him and you know it," I snap, crossing my arms over my chest.

"I do," he says.

"And you're still going to do it?" I ask.

"I am," he says, pulling his arm back from my shoulders. "I must. It is my duty."

"Your duty is to your family," I say.

"Yes," he says. "But we must eat. I must provide for you and for Malcolm."

"For us, sure, but why all the masses? You could hunt for us by yourself. Go outside the City and not risk exposure," I argue.

His brow furrows deeply as he frowns. "Amara..."

He doesn't finish his thought, snapping his mouth shut. He shakes his head and stands up without a word and walks towards our room.

"Is that it?" I say, my voice rising.

"What do I say, my love?" he asks.

"You say yes! You say that you'll not risk your family! That you won't do this," I say. "You're putting us on the line for them. It's not fair. Let the masses out there get their own damn food. Maybe they'd appreciate it more if they had to work for it."

He doesn't turn around while I yell at him. His shoulders slump, his head hangs down to his chest and his tail goes still. When I finish, he looks over his shoulder, but not at me.

"My love, I cannot do this," he says.

"I'm your treasure! You always tell me you'll do anything for me. This! This is what I want."

"Amara, please, do not do this," he says.

"Damn it, Shidan, I'm scared!" now my voice cracks, and the tears I've been fighting fall free. I wipe my sleeve across my face so rough it hurts my nose, which pisses me off even more. "You can't make light of this."

He turns around at last. His eyes are soft, and a frown is on his face, but he shakes his head.

9

"My dearest treasure, I am not," he says. "You know I cannot fail to do this. I have responsibilities."

"I'm your responsibility! Malcolm is your responsibility!"

"Yes," he agrees. "This is true."

"So stay!"

He closes his eyes, and I know he's counting to ten because it's a trick I taught him as I've been working to control my own temper. At last he shakes his head.

"I'll leave Malcolm home," he says. "But what we are doing now matters. It is the future we are creating."

"You're putting our future at risk," I counter, rising to my feet, balling my hands into fists. "I... I can't do this without you."

He crosses the space between us in one long stride and wraps his arms around me. I stiffen, holding myself tight, not ready to let go of my anger. If I let the anger go, I'll have nothing left to hold off the fear bubbling beneath it.

He squeezes me tight and my face rests against the coolness of his chest. He doesn't say a word, holding me tight until I can't keep the anger any longer. As it fades away my body melds to his and the fear bubbles out and over. Tears stream down my face as the yawning black swallows me into the pits of despair.

I'm sobbing against his chest. The one thing I've done my best not to do. I don't want Malcolm to see this—he won't understand. No matter how scary, it is a parent's job is to make the world as safe as possible.

This though, there is no fighting this. It's not like Invaders or Zzlo or even a zemlja. At least those you can see coming. I can fight those. This... this is silent. Invisible. Dangerous in ways we don't even comprehend.

"Shhh," he says, rubbing my back as he holds me.

"Mommy?" Malcolm asks.

Damn it. I pull out of Shidan's arms and run my hands

across my face, wiping away the tears the best I can. It's not going to hide that I've been crying. My face and eyes are puffy and fresh tears are threatening right behind the ones I cleaned off.

"Yes, love," I sniffle, hiding behind Shidan's bulk while I try to pull myself together.

"What's wrong, Mommy?" he asks. "Why are you scared?"

"I'm not scared, honey," I say. "We talked about what's happening outside and why you can't play with Illadon or Rverre right now."

"Sure," he says. "I told you it's going to be fine. Sure, bad things will happen, but we'll be okay, eventually."

I snort. Malcolm is always practical. He's so tiny, still my baby boy, and yet too often he's wiser than all of us. Especially me.

"You did," I agree.

"Don't you trust me?" he asks.

He walks around his dad and stares at me with an intensity that I've never seen from another living being. When he does this, I always feel like I'm on the spot. As if I were to lie to him, he would know it. I think, sometimes, he does, though he hasn't ever called me out for it.

"I do," I say, kneeling in front of him.

"Okay, Mommy," he says. "Don't worry. Tajss has a plan."

"Malcolm," I say, placing my hands on his tiny shoulders. "You know I don't like it when you talk like that. You can believe in things for yourself. You don't have to say that Tajss told you. You can know on your own."

"Sure, Mommy," Malcolm says, shrugging. "But I'm not going to lie to you either."

"Thank you, baby," I say, pulling him into a hug.

I crush him against my chest. I don't want to let him go. The world outside is terrifying, and I can't do anything about it. It's enough to drive any mother nuts.

"Too tight!" he exclaims, squirming his way out of my grip and dropping to the floor.

"Okay, go play," I say.

"Okay," he says, then stops in the doorway to his room. When he turns back, he has a faraway look on his face. "I'll stay home."

"You will?" I ask. "I thought you wanted to go?"

"Yeah," he says, shaking his head. His eyes focus back on the here and now, and his shoulders slump. "I guess I'll stay."

I look at Shidan, who gives me a subtle shake of his head to indicate he doesn't understand this change either.

"Okay baby, thank you," I say.

"Sure," he says, turning around, tail limp and dragging as he mopes his way into his room.

"What was that?" I ask.

"Our child is in tune with the planet," Shidan says. "Beyond that, I do not know."

Not an answer, but I don't have one either. Shidan slips the leather straps that will hold his lochaber over his arms and around his wings. I watch, silent. My stomach churns uncomfortably and pressure pounds in my head.

"Is there anything I can say?" I ask at last, and he stops to look at me.

"Amara," he says, taking hold of my upper arms. He stares into my eyes with an overwhelming care and intensity. "I love you. You truly are my everything, but you need to believe. Our love is one that goes beyond anything the stars themselves can count. My love for you is eternal. Nothing can ever tear us apart. I won't let it."

"But what if..." I trail off. I can't say it. Can't even think it.

He kisses my forehead then wraps his arms around me one last time. If only he would understand what I'm feeling. There's a certainty, I feel it in my bones, I'm certain something terrible is about to happen. It's barreling down on us like an incoming enemy ship and I have to stop it. But I can't see it to do anything about it. I can't even put it into words.

"There is no "what if," my treasure," he says softly.

"You don't know that," I disagree. "You could... anything could..."

My throat closes, and no more words will come. Anger is so much better than these depths of despair. All I can imagine is a nebulous future where I've lost him, my perfect Shidan. The man I never saw coming who is now the man I can't live without.

"I will be careful," he says. "This I promise you. I will do all I can to be safe."

"You better," my voice squeaks as I force the words out.

I hug him tighter. He holds me in silence, giving me this moment, because that's the man he is. Perfect. Patient. Giving. My everything, damn it all. He's my everything, and letting him go right now is the hardest thing I've ever had to do.

All my life has been hard choices, but none of them compare. I force my arms to relax. The muscles resist, some primal instinct urging me to not let him go. Scared of what I don't know, but a total certainty something awful is about to happen.

"I will, my love," he says.

I let go of him. Silent, I watch him finish attaching the harness across his chest. Then he slides his lochaber into place between his wings. He opens the door, steps into it, and stops. He turns and his radiant smile is on his face.

"I love you" bursts out of me.

"And I you, my treasure," he says.

The door closes, and I stand, staring, until Malcolm calls for me. Reluctantly, I turn away from the closed door, knowing, deep in my bones, something terrible is going to happen.

2

SHIDAN

*T*he City is quiet. Strange to think it's only been a couple of years, a blink of an eye really, since quiet was my normal and sound would be the unusual.

Until four days ago, though, the City wasn't bustling with sound, but it felt... alive. Now it feels empty. Alone. No one is moving on the streets, no banging as people work to clean out debris from the buildings. No construction. No conversation.

It's a sobering situation, and despite my attempt to keep it light with Amara, I am worried too. Ladon hasn't woken up, and while I've tried to keep it from her, Ormarr is getting worse too. While Ladon is in a coma, Ormarr is extremely sick and aggressive, though conscious.

Rosalind ordered the quarantine, but was it in time?

All I know now is that the two males are sick, but then I haven't seen anyone else since. Are more of us sick? When I've gone to get supplies from Bert, he passes on the latest news, but it's more rumor than fact.

According to Bert, more Zmaj have fallen ill, but he doesn't have names. Some of the humans he said have 'flu'-like symptoms, but I don't know what that means. I'd like to ask Amara but if I do, she'll want to know why I want to know. Too many questions would come of that.

I have to protect her, even if I'm protecting her from herself. She worries too much.

Someone emerges from a building across the street from me and stops. I wave, looking to see if I know them, but it's a human I don't recognize. They're carrying a large bag under one arm and have a piece of cloth wrapped around their head and covering most of their face.

"Hello," I call, waving.

The human, I think it's a male, backs through the door he came out of and disappears. Under normal circumstances, I'd investigate further. These are not normal times. It makes my scales itch to walk away from a mystery, but I promised Amara.

He probably didn't want to risk exposing himself. Bert said that most of the humans are afraid too, like Amara. How can I blame them? There is no way to fight this except hope you don't get it. We don't even know if it's deadly or if it will pass.

It's strange for a Zmaj to get sick. Rare, even. I dimly recall being ill to my stomach ages ago, but that's because I ate meat that had turned bad and I missed it. I was ill then, but nothing like what they say of this. I did not fall into a coma.

They say Ladon had a fever. That's weirdest of all, and I can only imagine it because Amara described it for me. Our physiology is cold-blooded—we don't get fevers. If anything, we love the warmth. We're products of Tajss, a desert planet. Warmth has always been my friend. I prefer it to being cold. Now I'm supposed to be afraid of being warm?

Bah. Ridiculous.

I stretch out my stride until my muscles twinge with the effort. It's so good to be outside. I wish I could have brought Malcolm. It's not good for him to be pent up inside. He needs sunshine, fresh air, and room to work his muscles. He's growing so big and strong. My heart swells, and I can't stop the smile on my face.

Amara is my treasure, my love, but Malcolm is my pride. He's so wise for his few years, but rambunctious as any good male should be. Ready to fight, to go to war, to protect what is his. He is a stunningly brilliant child.

My thoughts turn to Calista. I should check on her and make sure she and Illadon are okay. She is without her male. I'm sure some of our community are keeping in touch with her, but I want to do it myself. I owe that and so much more to Ladon.

How could I look him in the eye when he recovers—and he will recover—if I hadn't done all I could to make sure his female and his child are being cared for? I'll stop by on my way home. If I knock on the door then move to the end of the hallway, I won't risk exposure, but I'll also know that Calista has anything she needs.

Satisfaction warms my heart. I'm turning the last corner before the airlock and come to a stop. One of the males who stands guard is sitting at the airlock. Before I see him, I hear him coughing. He doesn't look well. His skin is a pasty white color. More of the moisture they call sweat than is normal is beaded on his forehead.

"Hello," I call, staying at the corner.

He coughs hard into his elbow before looking up. "What?" He's wheezing and looks ready to pass out.

"You do not look well, friend," I say.

"No shit?"

"No," I say. "It would be wise for you to get medical attention."

"Yeah, too bad we don't have a doctor," he says, coughing harshly into his elbow again.

"We have Addison," I say. "She will help you."

"She can't do nothing," he says. "Done saw her. She doesn't

16

know any more than anyone else. Told me I'm sick, like I didn't already know that."

"Then you should be in bed," I call down to him. "Rest is good for humans who do not feel well."

"That's what she said too," he said, coughing again. "But who's going to watch the door?"

"I am sure it will be fine," I say, shaking my head.

"You're not Rosalind," he says. "I take my orders from her."

"No," I agree. "I'm not, but I need to go outside to meet the Tribe. They do not know about the quarantine, and the grain delivery is today."

"Well, what's stopping you?" he asks, waving his free hand as he coughs into his other elbow.

"I do not wish to be rude, but I cannot risk being exposed to what you have," I say. "I'm sure you'll understand some precautions, in accordance with the quarantine."

"Fine," he huffs.

He stands up, weaves back and forth and it takes every ounce of my will not to rush forward to steady him. He places a hand on the softly humming dome and steadies himself then pushes off and shuffles a few strides away.

"Thank you," I say, moving to the airlock.

"Sure," he says between coughs.

I reach for the pad to open it but stop before I touch it. *Careful. Do not touch things that might be infected.* I pull a piece of cloth out of my pocket and wipe the pad down before using it. The continued coughing from over my shoulder makes my scales crawl. Is this the flu that Addison told me of? It looks miserable, and I feel for the man to be suffering so.

The door to the airlock swishes open. I step in, letting the automatic cycles do their work as the door closes and the air pressure is normalized again. Finally it opens on the other side out into the desert.

I step out into the blessed heat and lean my head back,

basking in the warmth. It's amazing. I want to throw myself into the loose sand and roll around. If Malcolm was with me, I would. The best part of being a father is getting to act like a child with no one judging you.

I smile as I think about my son. I never considered this life would be mine. Before Amara, I was resigned. I knew I would die, alone, and the only purpose in life was to live. That is no life at all. Living for the sake of oneself is no reason to carry on, yet I did. Drawn forward by something. Only now do I know it was her.

Some part of me, so deep I wasn't aware of it, must have known she was in my future. That Malcolm was. My son who will one day be a prophet. A seer such as I dimly recall existing before the Devastation.

Resisting my instinct to roll in the sand, I climb the nearest dune. When I reach the crest, I close the outer lenses of my eyes and stare across the desert, looking for the incoming Tribe members. I spot them, but they are further away than I would have thought. Either I am early or they're running behind. Glancing at the two suns tells me that they're not on time.

It's fine. I wait, wiggle my toes in the soft, hot sand, letting it cover my feet. The warmth soaks into my scales, and I close my eyes, enjoying the sensation.

The only thing that would make this moment better is if Amara and Malcolm were with me. Malcolm would race down the dune and laugh. In my imagination I can hear him giggling. Amara would yell for him to be careful. She worries, sometimes too much, but it is her way of showing how much she cares. How big her heart is, so much that she embraces us with it.

The time passes, and the Tribe delegation comes closer. They're pulling a sled along behind them, loaded with grain for the bivo. The bivo are not happy being penned in. It's against their nature, but the theory is that in a couple of generations, they'll be adjusted to it.

I hope the theory is right. We need a reliable source of meat. The area around the City has been hunted out. We were having to travel days out to find prey, and that's not sustainable. Our population is growing, slowly, but still growing.

"Shidan!" Drosdan yells, waving as he approaches.

"Hold!" I call out, startled from my daydreaming.

I didn't realize how close they'd already gotten. Drosdan is huge, even for a Zmaj. His arms are massive trunks, like baoba trees attached to a body. He stops at the bottom of the dune I'm on.

"What is it?" he asks. "Has something happened to Ormarr?"

Ragnar, another Zmaj, steps up next to him, along with his mate, Olivia.

"Yes," I say. "We are under a quarantine. I do not want to risk exposing you in case I'm infected and don't know it yet."

"A quarantine?" Drosdan asks.

Olivia and Ragnar speak too softly for me to hear. Drosdan seems angry, his tail rising between his wings.

"Yes," I say. "Ladon was exposed to something and then became sick."

"Right, Ormarr came to help," Ragnar says.

"Yes, and he too fell sick," I say. "We are being careful. Rosalind and Visidion have ordered a lockdown. We are not to interact with each other, and we must keep a safe distance apart. Addison says it is a virus that is spreading by contact."

"This makes no sense!" Drosdan argues. "Zmaj don't spread diseases. We never have!"

"I understand," I say, trying to calm the anger flowing off of him.

His anger is hitting me with palpable waves, calling to my bijass, making me want to respond in kind.

"Then tell me what sense this makes!" Drosdan says. "We

sent Ormarr to help, but he is needed by the Tribe. Let me take him home with us as I intended."

"I cannot," I say, holding my hands up in front of myself. "I must obey the Commander."

"Visidion or Rosalind?" Drosdan growls.

"You know they are in agreement," I answer.

"I know they say they are," he snaps.

"Drosdan, that's not going to help," Ragnar says.

"Rosalind is good," Olivia says. "And Visidion is her mate. They wouldn't do this without being sure it was the best thing."

"Bah," Drosdan says, shaking his head.

"What is the sickness?" Olivia asks. "How does it present?"

"I'm told Ladon is in a coma," I say. "It started with a fever."

"A fever?" Drosdan interrupts. "Zmaj don't get fevers. This is some kind of trick. What game are you playing Shidan?"

"Trust me, this is not a game," I say, shaking my head.

The suspicion on his face is clear. He doesn't trust me, and he doesn't trust Rosalind. I know this, she knows it, but he's always come into line for his Commander, Visidion.

"Let us into the City," he says, walking forward.

"No," I say. "Drosdan, I cannot. This is no game."

"What was it that Ladon was exposed to?" he asks, stopping and throwing his arms wide.

Olivia and Ragnar stand at the bottom of the hill. They look from each other, to him, and then to me. They don't know what to do with him either. I don't know how to answer his question. I was briefed on what happened, but I don't know if I'm supposed to share that information broadly. If I tell Drosdan, then the entire Tribe will know it.

"I'm not sure," I lie. "Something in the desert."

"There is nothing in Tajss that will make a Zmaj sick!" Drosdan yells. "This is our home. Now give me back Ormarr, or I'm going to take him."

He moves again so I step backwards.

"Please, Drosdan," I say. "Do not do this. It is not wise."

"What is not wise is you standing in my way any longer, little male," he bellows as he storms his way up the dune, coming closer and closer.

"Drosdan!" I yell, but he doesn't stop.

I walk backwards, doing my best to keep the distance between us as Addison advised. He's crazed, and I'd rather not fight him under normal circumstances. I don't know how to fight him and keep a healthy distance between us.

I keep moving away from him. Finally, he rages past me, going up to the door to the airlock. He pounds on it with both fists.

"Let me in!" he roars, hitting the door over and over.

I'm not sure how much force that door can take. It's not part of the forcefield generator that makes the dome itself, it's a regular door. I'm sure it can't be good for it to have the giant oaf beating on it.

"Drosdan, stop," I say. "Ragnar, help me, please."

Ragnar looks at Olivia, and she nods emphatically to him. Ragnar runs past my position and up to Drosdan. He catches Drosdan by the wrist as he swings yet again at the door. Drosdan turns to face him, and I'm sure that he's about to hit him next.

"I am myself," Ragnar says.

Drosdan stops, his body trembling with the effort to contain himself.

"I *am* myself, "Ragnar repeats, almost growling the words.

"Together we are stronger," Drosdan responds, dropping his arms to his sides.

"Survival of the group matters," Ragnar finishes.

"Fine," Drosdan says, turning away from the door.

Even from here I can see there are new dents in the metal. The two males move away from the door towards me until I hold a hand up for them to stop.

"We're supposed to stay at least two wingspans apart," I say.

"Fine," Ragnar says. "When did this start?"

"How long is it for?" Olivia asks, coming up to stand with them.

"It started four days ago," I say. "Ladon got sick before that, and then when Ormarr caught it Rosalind ordered the lockdown."

"For how long?" Drosdan growls.

"I don't know." I say with a shrug.

"We can't risk returning this to the Tribe," Olivia says. "All the kids are there. Have any of the children here been exposed?"

I shake my head. "We don't think so at least. None of them are sick."

"That's a relief," Olivia says.

"It is," I agree.

"Your supplies are on the sled," Drosdan says. "We need it back though if we're going to bring your next batch of grains."

"Can you unload it by the door?" I ask. "Then I can get people to carry it to the bivo pens."

"Yes," Ragnar agrees. "What about our meat return?"

"It's waiting for you," I say. "We need to be careful on the loading, and you should take steps to sanitize everything we give you."

"With what?" Olivia asks. "We don't have electric cleansers like we had on the ship that kills germs."

I don't have a good answer to that. "You have soap?"

"Just what we make ourselves," she says.

"When you get back home, wash the outside of the packages with soap and water before you take them in," I say. Privately, I think we have to hope that the illness is not transferred that way. Maybe the sunlight shining on the packages as they travel will help.

"That will take forever!" Drosdan says.

"Yes, it will, Drosdan," Olivia says quietly. "It's worth it to keep the whole Tribe from getting sick. To keep Sarah from getting a fever and falling into a coma."

Drosdan blows out an angry breath, and his shoulders slump. The only time I have seen him purely peaceful is when he is with his mate, Sarah. He's not peaceful now when he turns to me, though.

"This better not be a joke," he says, his eyes narrowing.

"I wish it was," I say.

"Then let's get to work," Ragnar says. "This is going to take longer if we have to keep further apart."

It takes more time. I don't mind because being outside in the sun and working hard feels good. I'm getting to use muscles that even after only four days feel stiff and under-worked. The Tribe members keep their distance from me as I do them, and eventually, we finish the work.

We're standing two wingspans apart. Ragnar and Olivia hold hands behind Drosdan, who has his arms crossed over his chest and a deep frown.

"How long do you expect to keep Ormarr?" Drosdan asks.

"I don't know," I say. "I'm sure Addison will send him home as soon as possible."

"I'll let Bailey know what's happening," Olivia says.

"Thank you," I say.

"We'll be back in two cycles of Sestejan," Drosdan says.

Sestejan is the smaller of Tajss' two suns. In the humans' terms it would be the same as two of their weeks. Amara has been helping me to understand their different methods of measuring time and space. It's a study I find interesting.

"I will see you then," I say.

Drosdan grunts then slips the reigns of the sled over his shoulders and walks away. Olivia lingers behind. Ragnar steps away then stops, waiting on his mate.

"Shidan," Olivia says. "How bad is it?"

"It will all be fine," I assure her.

"Cut the bivoshit," she says, shaking her head. "Tell me true."

The intensity in her eyes is more than I can meet. I can't lie to her, and it's forcing me to be honest with myself, too.

"It's bad," I say at last. "We don't know more than that."

Her lips tremble as she nods and then turns and walks away. Ragnar puts an arm around her shoulders, and they walk side by side, climbing the first dune towards home. My own arms ache with emptiness, and I want nothing more than to have Amara in my arms.

I run for home.

3

AMARA - TWO WEEKS LATER

*S*unlight on my face wakes me up. I stretch and roll over. Shidan is still sleeping, so I slide closer and rest my head on his chest. His hearts beat slow and even, one echoing the other. His chest rises and falls, taking me up and down with each breath. I nestle a leg over his and close my eyes. He shifts and hooks his arm around my shoulders but doesn't wake up.

I drift in and out of sleep, enjoying the quiet. I doubt Malcolm is awake yet, or I'd hear him. If he is, he's entertaining himself in his room, and I don't want to miss the opportunity to be with Shidan without having to worry about our boy.

After a while he shifts, groans, then his eyes flutter open. He pulls me closer into a kiss. His lips are soft and pliable, inviting more. I move my leg up and down along his morning wood. He moans into our kiss.

"Good morning," he whispers.

"Morning," I say, running my hand down across his chest and down to his dick.

"Malcolm?" he asks.

"Sleeping," I shush him.

"Mmm," he moans, grabbing my hips.

He pulls me on top. I lift my hips and lean forward, placing my hands on either side of his head. He uses his free hand to position himself at my opening, moving it back and forth, teasing. I rest my forehead against his, closing my eyes and enjoying his touch.

The head slips in and I slide down onto his cock until he's fully seated. We kiss, his tongue pushing into my mouth, claiming it.

I rise up and slide down, enjoying him slowly.

He moans into our kiss. I rise up and lean back. Run my fingers through my own hair as I ride his dick. He grabs my tits and plays with them, teasing the nipples to hard points.

He puts one hand between us and teases my clit. I bite my lip to keep from crying out. I don't want to risk waking up Malcolm.

I ride his cock faster and faster. An orgasm is coming fast. I don't hold back. Dragging sex out is for people without little ones that might wake up at any time.

Shidan understands and doesn't hold back either. He drives in, forcefully seating himself with each thrust. In moments, an orgasm rips through me. My back arches and my toes curl as the sensation races through my center and out my limbs.

I collapse onto him, a quivering mess. He wraps his arms tight and holds me. He raises his head and looks at the door to our room. When he lies back down, a broad smile is on his face. He rolls us over, and in an instant his second cock is pushing into me.

"Oh!" I exclaim in surprise.

He doesn't slow down though. We don't know how long we're going to have to do this. It's rare to find enough time to go once, much less twice.

If our first run was making love, then this is hard-core fucking. He thrusts hard, grinds, pulls back, then thrusts again.

We buck against each other, driving hard until a fresh orgasm is dancing across our bodies and we come together, shuddering in each other's arms.

He drops beside me and peppers me with kisses.

"I love you," he says over and over between touches of his lips.

"I love you too," I say, squirming away when he tries to kiss my neck. "That tickles!"

"I can't help myself," he says. "You're ravishing. I must kiss every inch of you."

"You think so?" I laugh, rolling out of bed. "Because our son will be wanting breakfast any moment."

"Our son, who is as brilliant as his mother," he says.

"Thanks for noticing," I say, picking up clothes off the floor and pulling them on. "But I need to go make food."

"I should take him with me to the meeting," he says, resting his head on his arms while lying in bed.

"Are you serious?" I ask, stopping midway through pulling my shirt on.

"Sure," he says. "It will be good to get him out. Boy needs some sun."

"Shidan," I say. "We agreed two weeks ago that we'd keep him in and safe."

He frowns. "I don't recall this," he says.

"You don't recall?" I ask, staring at him, disbelief causing my mind to go blank.

"No."

"How can you not recall? It was a fight! You wanted to take him out. Shidan, I told you I was scared then, how can you even think about taking him out?"

"I'm sorry," he says. "It was only an idea."

"You remember that Ladon has gotten worse? He woke up, but he's regressed. He and Ormarr are both locked up for their own safety and that of others. They're deep in their bijass.

Addison is working day and night to find a cure, but so far nothing. How can you even think about taking our son out where he might be exposed? We talked about this!"

"Of course," he says, sitting up and turning his back. "I'm sorry I forgot."

I shut up but I can't quit staring at him. He forgot? Shidan never forgets anything. He remembers details of things I don't even notice. The idea of him forgetting an argument is unreal to me. Me, sure, but Shidan? No way, that's not him.

I walk over and put my hands on his cheeks, pulling his face up to look at me. He smiles.

"Are you okay?" I ask.

I'm subtly checking for fever because I'm concerned. I shouldn't be, but I am.

"I'm fine, my treasure," he says.

No fever. Okay, then it's probably nothing, right? Anyone can forget something. It happens. Shaking my head, I go back to my side of the bed and grab the rest of my clothes. He dresses himself while I finish pulling on my clothes. I open my mouth to say something about it when the door bursts open and Malcolm rushes into the room. Malcolm leaps from the doorway into the air, and Shidan catches him, whirls him around.

"My boy!" Shidan yells.

"Daddy!" Malcolm giggles, his little legs still pumping.

"Did you sleep well?" Shidan asks.

"I did," Malcolm says. "There were bad dreams, but it all works out okay. That's what you say."

"It is," Shidan agrees. He sets Malcolm onto his hip and turns towards me. "Mommy is awake too."

"Mommy!" Malcolm exclaims, reaching for me with wiggling fingers.

"Mommy has to fix breakfast, my little love," I say.

"Breakfast, yes, yes, yes," Malcolm says.

"Break-fast, break-fast, break-fast," Shidan chants and Malcolm joins him.

"Okay!" I laugh and head out for the kitchen.

"Do you need help, my love?" Shidan asks.

"I got it," I say, going past him.

"Okay," he says, then he zooms Malcolm through the air as if he's an airplane.

While they play together, I look through our pantry. I haven't forgotten the lapse in Shidan's memory. It could be nothing. Maybe. Or it could be something.

He doesn't have a fever, so that's good. It means everything is okay. I think. I hope. When I finish digging through the pantry, it's clear I've got bigger things to worry about than making something out of nothing.

Our food supply is low. Really low. I'm sure everyone in the City is feeling the pinch. Our food stocks have never been excessive at the best of times. The supplies we salvaged from the wreckage of the generation ship have been dwindling to the point of non-existence, leaving us dependent on what we can farm and hunt.

That's why the bivo taming project is so important. We've over-hunted around the City itself and there's hardly anything left. The hunters must travel for days to find prey and then they have to get it back before it spoils. Or they stay out even longer to butcher and smoke the meats. Neither of which are an ideal scenario.

If we can domesticate the bivo herd, we'll have a steady supply of meat. The Tribe is progressing on growing vegetables and some fruits. By the time Malcolm grows up we should have the food supply handled, except there are a lot of ifs in that.

The quarantine has slowed everything. Basics are hard, if not impossible, to come by, and the Tribe has restricted their trips here to every other week. Our supplies were for only a week here in the house, but I haven't wanted to go out. I can't put my boys at risk.

Sighing, I pull together some grains and pieces of smoked guster and throw them all into a pan. I bend over to try to light the flame on the makeshift stove.

It's not really a stove, or not a normal one as I'd like. I guess it's normal for Tajss. It's really a box made of hardened clay. There's an opening on the front where I put kindling, which is how I prefer to think of it, since it's actually dried bivo droppings. I prefer to not think about the idea that my food is being cooked over poo. Gross.

Starting a fire isn't easy though. We don't have matches and the lighters we did have ran out of fuel long ago. I have a clay bowl that I fill with flammable kindling and two stones that spark when I strike them. If I do everything right, hold my breath for the exact length of time, and the gods of fortune smile, I can start a fire relatively quick.

Normally it takes me a while, and today, unfortunately, is normal. It'd be easier to ask Shidan to come in and do his breathing fire trick, but I can still hear him and Malcolm laughing. I don't want to interrupt them, so I bang the stones together again. And again. And again.

"Damn stones," I mutter under my breath slamming them together with more force.

"Ouch!" I yell, as I smash my thumb between the stones. I drop them both but at the same time the kindling catches fire. Of course.

"Amara?" Shidan calls emerging from the bedroom. "Are you okay, my love?"

"Fine," I call. "Trying to light the stove."

"Let me help," he says.

"I got it now," I say, then turn back and see that the kindling I had lit has burned out, leaving me back at square one. "Uh, maybe I don't."

"I will help," he says, striding into the kitchen with his sexy, arrogant confidence.

Malcolm tumbles along behind him, doing his best to imitate his dad, but his tiny legs aren't steady enough yet to match up.

Shidan kneels in front of the opening beneath the stove and inhales deeply. He belches, loudly, and a burst of flame shoots from his mouth into the opening. There's a loud whoosh as the poo catches on fire, but something happens. A ball of orange flame blasts out of the hole back into Shidan's face.

He stumbles backwards exclaiming loudly, patting at his face. The scent of singed hair fills the room, and I run over to him.

"Are you okay?" I ask.

"Fine," he snaps, running his hands over his face.

"Let me see," I say.

"I said I was fine!" he snaps.

I take a step back and bump up against Malcolm. Malcolm grabs my leg and squeezes tight. I pick him up, swing him onto my hip, and take another step back from Shidan. He's never, in all our time together, snapped at me like that.

My lip trembles, and my throat is closed tight. He doesn't seem to even notice. He shakes his head, runs his hands through his hair, then at last turns to look at Malcolm and me.

"What is the matter?" he asks.

I swallow, working the lump out of my throat before I can speak.

"You're okay?" I ask.

"Yes," he says. "That was surprising, though."

"Yeah," I agree.

"What's the matter?" he asks, frowning as he takes a step towards us. Instinctively I take a step backwards, and Malcolm clings to my neck tighter. "Amara?"

He looks confused, and there is no hint of the anger in his

face or posture, but it doesn't change what he did. That which he's never, ever done.

"Are you sure you're okay?" I ask.

"Of course my love, what is the matter?"

"You snapped at me," I say.

"I did?" he asks, brow furrowing.

"Shidan, don't you remember? It happened a minute ago."

"I was surprised, that's all," he says. "The fire blew into my face. It was nothing."

"Sure," I say, but I'm only being agreeable.

It wasn't nothing. It was a long way from nothing. Cold fingers stretch out from my core.

"Mommy," Malcolm says.

"It's fine honey," I lie. "Daddy was surprised, that's all."

I can't quit staring at Shidan, but the remorse on his face is so clear, and this is so out of character for him, I don't know what to do or say.

"I'm sorry," Shidan says, shaking his head. He runs his hands over his hair again, frowning. "That really shocked me."

I set Malcolm down. "Go play."

Our son runs off to his room, and I walk over to Shidan. I place a hand on his forehead and one on his chest.

"I'm fine," he says. "I don't know what that was, but I'm okay."

"Right," I say. "Shidan, this isn't normal. Something is happening. I want you to get checked out by Addison."

He frowns then nods. "I will. After I check on the bivo and take the delivery today."

"Fine," I say. "But do it. I'm worried."

I drop my voice before I say the last, not wanting Malcolm to overhear me.

"Of course my love," he says, kissing my forehead. "I am sorry."

"It's fine," I say, stirring the food in the skillet. The tangy smell drifts out as it warms. "While you're gone, I'm going to check on Calista. I can't imagine what she's going through."

"Be careful," Shidan says.

"Of course," I say. "I'll maintain quarantine, but I want her to know she's not alone."

"A good idea," Shidan says. "Is Illadon with her still?"

"I don't know," I say. "If he is, I might offer to take him to Jolie. I don't know how I'd handle Malcolm if anything was to happen to you and care for you at the same time. It might be the best help I can give."

"Be careful my love," he says. "That is all I ask."

"It's all I ask of you too," I say. "Don't be a hero, okay?"

He smiles, getting out plates and setting them on the counter. I dip the food up and we sit down to have our meal as a family. If only I knew this was the moment before everything changed. I would burn it into my memory, somehow. The future doesn't broadcast itself to us though.

"We have to stand at the end of the hallway," I remind Malcolm again.

"I know, Mommy," he huffs, hustling to keep up with me.

"I could carry you," I say.

"No," he shakes his head leaning into his walk even more. "I got this."

He's so determined, and I don't want to take that away from him, so I let him walk. His little face is red, his cheeks puffing in and out, despite the fact I've been keeping my steps slow. He'll make it. He's tough.

When we reach Calista's building, I don't give him any more choice about the stairs. He's pushed himself hard enough as it is. We reach her apartment and I knock, then retreat to the end of the hall. It's a long time before the door opens and Calista looks out. Her face is pale, and eyes are red and puffy.

"Calista," I say, pulling her attention to the end of the hall where Malcolm and I are.

"Oh, hey," she says, smiling wanly.

"I came to see if there's anything you need," I say.

She snorts and shakes her head. "A miracle?"

There's a loud crash from the apartment, and she jumps, letting out a yelp. "Illadon?"

"I'm fine, Mommy," he says. A moment later he sticks his head out the door. "Who's he—Malcolm!"

"Hi, Illadon," Malcolm says, waving enthusiastically.

"Any word yet?" I ask Calista.

"No," she shakes her head. "It's worse, if anything."

"Oh honey, I'm so sorry," I say.

Calista shrugs and shakes her head. "It's not your fault. Nothing we can do, right?"

"I'm sure Addison will come up with a cure," I say. "She needs time, that's all."

"Time," Calista says. "That's one thing I have in spades."

"I understand," I say. "Would you like me to take Illadon to Jolie?"

Calista looks down at Illadon who bounces up and down. "Yes!"

"Would you mind?" Calista asks. "He's been pent up here too long. He needs someone to play with."

"I want to play, too," Malcolm says.

"I know dear," I say. "Illadon, pack a bag and I'll take you to Jolie."

"Be right back!" Illadon says, running into the apartment.

"Do you need anything else?" I ask. "Food? Water?"

"I'm fine," Calista says. "Everyone has been very helpful. I'd like to go back to work but I've been directly exposed, and Addison is certain that humans are acting as a carrier."

"But nothing on the kids, right?" I ask.

"Right. She says they seem to be completely immune. They're not passing it on at all, though how she knows that for sure, I don't know."

"We have to trust in her," I say.

"How's the bivo project coming?" Calista asks, shoulders slumping as she leans against the wall next to the door.

Her eyes are glassy and she has a faraway look on her face. My heart breaks looking at my friend. Every instinct screams for me to go and hug her. I can't.

"Fine," I say. "Calista, I'm so sorry. I want to… I want to hug you. I want to make this all go away. I want to fix it."

She smiles. A real smile, the smile of the old Calista. The one I know and love, even if it's only a shadow of herself.

"I know," she says. "Amara the ass-kicker."

"Well, yeah," I say, shuffling my feet.

"You know Jolie and I joke about you, right?"

"No," I say, cheeks warming.

"Yeah, we always say if something needs done, put Amara on it. She'll get it done no matter who she has to bowl over to make it happen."

"Thanks, I think," I say.

She sighs. "It is a compliment. Really. You've always been the most headstrong of us girls."

"Well," I say, shaking my head uncertain what to say. "I appreciate it."

"I appreciate you," she sighs hanging her head. "I never… I never thought I'd be without him, you know? I mean how weird is all of this? We crash here, of all the godforsaken places in the universe, and we meet our guys. I know the boys are all about fate and meant to be together, but this is one hell of a string of coincidences isn't it?"

"Yes, it is," I say.

"But even so…" she trails off, drumming her fists against the wall. "I can't do it alone."

"You're not alone," I say. "And he's coming back to you. I know it, in my bones, I know."

"I think so," she says, but it's barely a whisper. "I hope so."

"He will," I promise. "He has to. Fate isn't that cruel."

"I'm ready!" Illadon says, bounding out of the door. "Bye, Mom!"

He grabs Calista and pulls her into a hug. He's half as tall and then some as Calista already. He's going to have his father's build for sure, but I can absolutely see Calista in him. His nose, the eyes, and the leanness to his muscular build.

"Listen to Amara and Jolie," Calista says, holding him by his shoulders. "Be good, don't tear things up."

"I will and I won't," he says. "Dad will be fine soon. I'm sure of it. He's the greatest warrior of all. He'll beat this thing soon."

"You're right, my love," Calista says. "You're right."

"Of course I am!" he declares puffing his chest out. "Let's go!"

He runs down the hall and Malcolm bounces as he approaches. "Illadon!"

"I'll check on you soon," I say before I turn away.

Calista nods and gives me the wan smile before disappearing into her apartment and shutting the door. There's a heavy finality as the door closes that makes my heart ache. If I worry about her enough than I won't have to think about Shidan and what happened this morning.

He doesn't have a fever. He's okay. He hasn't been exposed.

The boys chase each other out of the building and through the streets as I herd them toward Jolie. It takes a lot longer than it should, but they have a grand time. They chase each other, play hide and seek around objects, tag, and some other games of their own devising that I couldn't possibly understand the rules of, if it has rules at all.

At last we make our way to Jolie's apartment. I order the boys to wait at the end of the hall, knock, then move to rejoin them before the door opens. When Jolie comes out, she smiles.

"Amara! Boys!" she says.

"Boys?" Rverre calls from inside the apartment.

"How are you, Jolie?" I ask.

"We're getting by," she says. "Sverre is going nuts, but you know, other than that."

"It's hard being cooped up this long," I say.

"Yeah," she says. "Boys, did you come to play?"

"Yes!" they yell in unison.

"Go on in," she says. "Sverre and Rverre are in the kitchen."

"Snacks?" Illadon asks as he races by.

"Of course," Jolie says, leaning on the door frame.

"How's Shidan?" she asks.

I bite my lip hard, fighting against the sudden surge of tears threatening to break free. I force a smile, but my vision is blurring.

"Fine," I lie.

"What's happened?" she asks, straightening up.

The emotional storm roiling inside locks me up. I can't think, can't speak, can't force the words out. Jolie moves, stops, raises her arms, then drops them helplessly to her side.

"He's… I don't know… he… something," I sputter. Jolie nods encouragingly. "He snapped at me and he forgot something that happened two weeks ago."

It sounds stupid when I say it. What couple doesn't have spats every now and then? Who doesn't forget something? Except Shidan never has. We've been together for three years or more and he's never done it. Not once.

Sure we've had disagreements, we've argued, but never snapping at one another. Never like he acted. And forget something? Not Shidan.

"When did it start?" Jolie asks, not making light of my fears.

I'm so grateful that I take a step forward before stopping myself, wanting with all my heart to hug her.

"Shit, this quarantine sucks," I grumble.

"Right?" Jolie asks, raising her arms and giving me a long-distance hug. "I'm sorry. I want to hug you so much, but..."

She trails off, shrugging.

"I know," I say. "Thank you. It only just started."

"Has he been exposed? Any chance?" she asks.

"I don't know," I say. "He's still going out to care for the bivo, and he's been the Zmaj going to meet the Tribe when they deliver supplies. It's possible."

"Has he seen Addison?" she asks.

"No, he's supposed to go see her today though," I say.

"Good, make sure he does," she says. She frowns, scratches her head, and looks at her feet. "I could ask Sverre to handle the bivo."

Her voice is heavy with worry. She doesn't want to put her man at risk either, but she's offering because that's Jolie. She's kind to a fault and her heart is so big she will give the shirt off her back.

"No," I say shaking my head. "Not yet. Let's see what Addison says."

"Thankfully, the kids aren't carrying it," she says.

"Right?" I agree. "There's at least one thing to be thankful for."

"How's Calista?" she asks.

We talk about Calista and catch each other up on the latest news that we know. I'm giving Malcolm all the time I can since I haven't been letting him out of the house at all. He needs the time with others I'm sure, and I'm glad to have her to talk with. It puts my mind onto other things besides my own worries. A girl can stare at the same four walls for only so long. I need to see other people, sometimes at least.

Eventually we run out of things to talk about but neither of us seem in a hurry to end our time together, distant though it might be. When we've run completely out of things to talk about, I hold up my hands and shake my head.

"I got nothing," I admit.

Jolie smiles and shakes her head. "Me either."

"Mind sending Malcolm back out?"

"Sure," she says. "So, another couple weeks?"

"Sounds like a plan," I say, and she disappears into her apartment to retrieve my son.

As silence fills the hallway around me the weight of worry settles back onto my shoulders, but it doesn't seem as heavy. At least now I feel less alone than I did. Shidan will be all right. He has to be. I can't imagine my world without him.

4

SHIDAN

"*N*o," I call out. "Don't do that!"

Al is sitting astride the rock wall of the pen I helped design for the bivo. He's about to jump down on the side with the bivo, which is a terrible idea. Dangerous for him. He's a human and not strong enough to stop a bivo if one of them was to charge him.

"I got this," he says.

"No!" I yell again, running towards him, but he drops inside the pen.

I can only see the top of his head on the other side. I drop the bag of grains I'm carrying to move faster. There's a low moan as the bivo alpha notices the intruder. This is bad.

"Back off, cow!" Al yells.

"Al, don't threaten it!" I call out, but it's too late.

The stampeding sound of hoof beats comes over the stone wall. Al's hand appears over the top, and then his head. His eyes are wide with terror, his face red with exertion. I grab his hands and jerk him over. An instant later, the wall reverberates hard as the alpha slams into it where Al was a moment ago.

Al drops to the ground, panting and shaking. I step back,

only now taking time to realize I've broken quarantine. If Al is carrying the illness, I'm exposed. The bijass surges over my thoughts and my vision takes on a red haze.

"Why did you not listen?!" I yell.

Al looks up at me from the ground, and now his eyes are wide with fresh fear. He raises his arms defensively.

"I thought I could—"

"You didn't think!" I yell, throwing my arms wide.

My hands ball into fists. I want to hit him, hit something, anything. A target for the rage, anything to release it. Get it out.

I turn my back on the human and storm away. The primal fog ebbs and swells through my thoughts, assaulting my control. Muttering, I thunder across the open sands with nothing to exact my anger against.

I turn and look back where I came from. On the far side of the wall, the bivo alpha stares. It stomps the ground, glaring with bloodshot eyes. It snorts, shaking its head. My hands balled into fists, tail straight up behind me, I spread my wings and growl.

It paws the sand and snorts loudly, rumbling a challenge. I run at the wall. My feet pound the sand as I tilt my wings to catch the air, lightening my weight. When I'm one stride from the wall, I leap and easily glide over it. I land inside the pen and throw my arms wide, roaring my challenge to the bivo.

It roars back and charges. I don't wait for its approach, I run for it too. I cock my fist back, and when it's in range I swing, punching for its forehead. My fist glances off the hard bone of its skull, and the alpha slams into me. The wind rushes out of me, and I'm knocked backwards, flying through the air.

CRACK!

I hit the stone wall of the enclosure. Stars dance in my head, and the bijass swells, primal instincts taking over. The alpha backs up, pawing the ground and snorting, preparing for another charge.

It runs, thundering forward, so I roll to one side.

It hits the wall with a resounding force, the tusks and horns scraping against the stone. I grab the horns and twist, forcing its head to one side. It fights against me and I roar, accepting its challenge.

It twists its head back and forth and I lose my grip. It runs away, putting distance between us. The herd it's protecting huddles on the far side of the large enclosure, docilely awaiting the outcome.

Shaking my head I try to clear the stars still dancing in my vision. The fog over my thoughts leaves me seeing red as they slowly pass. The alpha paws the ground, preparing a fresh charge.

A smile spreads across my face. A challenge. An opponent to be vanquished.

"Get out of there!" the human male yells, but I ignore him.

He is weak. I'm the dominant male by far.

The alpha charges, and I run too. The ground rumbles as we race towards one another, the distance closing fast. The bivo's head grows larger and larger, dominating my vision. It lowers its head and when it does, I leap.

With my wings spreading, I glide up and over the top of its head. As I pass above it, I slam the thick part of my tail between its eyes. There's a loud crack, a mewl, and the alpha drops.

I close my wings and drop on top of it. I place my foot on it and roar to the suns above challenging one and all. None can stand against me. I am the dominant predator of Tajss.

Inside the raging storm of the bijass I see myself acting, but I can't stop myself. I exert myself, fighting to take control, and at last, I'm able to push the fog down. Mentally I climb out of the bijass.

The human male appears on the far side of the wall as the bivo herd moves closer, mewling in acceptance of their new alpha. The human male stares with his jaw slack and eyes wide.

"Are you okay?" he asks.

Shaking my head to clear the last of the fog away, I try to answer, but the words don't come out. I know words, there is one I should say but I can't recall it. I snap my mouth shut and nod instead. Words. What are the words?

Oh!

"Fine," I say, walking towards him.

Something has changed. Something is missing but I can't put my finger on what. There's an emptiness in my thoughts that resonates deep in my soul, but whatever it is, I can't remember, and it doesn't seem that important, really.

"That was incredible," the human male says.

"Who are you?" I ask.

The frown on his face and the way he works his mouth makes me think I've said something wrong. He finally shakes his head.

"I'm Al," he says. "You know me, Shidan. Why are you acting like you don't?"

"Of course I do," I say, but the name means nothing to me. The emptiness in my thoughts pulses like maybe I should know him.

My scales itch and I can't stand the way he's looking at me, so I jump the wall and walk closer to him.

"Woah!" he says, holding his hands up. "Don't forget the quarantine. We have to keep our distance."

"Right," I say, but I have no idea what he's talking about.

Amara. Malcolm. My mate and my child. Images of them drift to the forefront of my thoughts. I need to get back to them. They are mine to protect. I don't know why I'm out here without them, but a male should never leave his mate unprotected. It isn't wise.

"I can finish here if you want," Al says.

I stare at him trying to decide what he means. What is it he wants to finish here? I look around and there is no meat to butcher, no hides to tan. There is nothing but this strange wall of harvested stone penning in a herd of bivo. Why anyone would want to wall in a herd of bivo is beyond me, but if this human wants to 'finish' it then why would I stop him?

"Sure," I agree. "I'm going back to my mate."

I don't know why I bother telling him that. It seems like the right thing to do, and more than anything, it slipped out without thinking about it. I turn my back on the human and walk back towards... what?

A City lies in front of me covered by a glimmering dome. A dome... right, home. This is my home. I stride across the desert. Amara. I have to get to Amara.

I can see her face. Smell the scent of her hair. She's what matters. I reach the airlock to enter the City and touch the pad for entry. The code is... I know it. It's...

"Let me help," the human male says, appearing out of nowhere.

I jump to one side, tail rising between my wings and hands balling into fists.

"Hey, I'm helping," the human says.

"Right," I say, forcing my tail back down and unclenching my fists.

He enters a code while I watch, and the moment he does, I recall it. I think. I knew it but now that I recognized it its gone. Running my hands through my hair, I try to push the fog away, but it doesn't help.

"Thanks," I say, as the door swishes open and we walk in.

"That was amazing, by the way," the male says.

What was his name? I can't recall it. I know it, I know I know it. It's right there, but it won't come through.

"Heh," I grunt.

"Never seen anyone take out an alpha like that," he continues while we wait on the airlock to cycle. The space is too small. Despite the fact that I can see through it all the way around, I want out. It's too close.

"Heh," I say again, balling my fists.

Amara. Home. I have to get home. My scales itch, the fog in my head surges, and the space is closing in on me. I shift from foot to foot, tail twitching. Finally the inner door opens, and I push the human male out of the way to get out.

"Hey," he exclaims, but I ignore him and rush down the street.

The street is empty. The buildings are broken and decaying. The streets themselves are in bad repair, filled with holes that should have been repaired if anyone was caring for the area. Where are all the people?

The air is thick, hot, it's hard to breathe. Home is here, somewhere. I come to an intersection and stop. The buildings on each corner are tall, five or six stories each. Once they had windows, but those are all busted, leaving yawning dark openings that could be hiding anything. Creatures could be hiding in those dim places. Waiting, testing to see if I'm strong enough.

Is my home here? It feels like it is. I feel Amara. I know her and I have to get back to her. Her and my son. My son. He needs me. Why did I leave them?

I can't recall which direction is the way home, so I decide on an unclear instinct to go right. I walk down the middle of the road while the scales on the back of my neck itch. It feels like I'm being watched though nothing dares to challenge me.

Why can't I remember? I thought home was this way but now nothing looks familiar. I don't know these places. These empty, broken buildings are not places I know. They're not home. And above all, there is no sign of Amara.

"Amara!" I yell.

My own voice echoes back, taunting me.

This doesn't make sense. Where is she? Has something

45

happened? Why is this all different than it was? Where are the other... who?

Anger surges along with the fog, and I run. My feet slap against the material of the street, my tail dragging along it, the only sounds. I run for blocks until the dome comes back into sight ahead.

This isn't right. The dome shouldn't be there. I've gone the wrong way.

Turning back around, I stare down the empty street. The suns are dropping towards the horizon casting a dimming amber light. Frowning, I search for any sign, something familiar, anything that calls me towards her.

Nothing.

None of this looks like anything I know. Fine, I close my eyes. She is my treasure, my soul knows her, she is mine. I know where mine is, so I reach out and try to feel my way to her. My hearts pound in my ears and nothing happens. I wait, breathing deeply and exhaling slowly.

I have to find Amara. My treasure. Where are you...

My hearts slow, the raging beating in my ears drops away and then there is only the sound of my breath in and out. She's ahead. I know it.

Opening my eyes, I walk. I'm not going to run this time. Running would be giving myself over to a panic. I'm not in a panic. I'm in control. My treasure calls to me. All I have to do is follow her song.

It is like the first time. When I saw the fire streak across the sky it was a sign. I knew in my heart that she was there waiting for me, though I didn't understand what was waiting, there was no resisting the urge to go. I knew the moment I saw her, she was meant to be mine. It took time, but the pursuit of her was the greatest hunt of my life. She is all that matters.

The empty streets echo my footsteps back at me. Hollow. It feels wrong. There should be... something? Someone? None of it seems familiar, yet I know on some level I know this place. Fog covers my thoughts if I try to remember, obscuring the pictures of the past.

I stop, rubbing the back of my neck as I turn in a slow circle. It's unusually warm today, and my neck itches. A slow burning sensation in my guts roils as anger builds inside me. I bare my teeth and choose a direction on instinct. It feels right, but nothing seems right.

I walk for blocks, holding to the one thing I know. Amara. Amara needs me. I need her.

As my anger builds, I begin running until I'm sprinting down the streets. A stitch forms in my side, and I push past it. My breath becomes ragged, and still I run. The muscles in my legs burn, and still I run.

The road forms a dead end, so I turn to the right and come to a halting stop. The dome shimmers at the end of the street. My hearts pound and I can't clear my head.

"No," I mutter, clenching and unclenching my hands. "AMARA!"

It rips out, tearing at my throat. Cold chills race down my arms. I can't find her. She's lost to me.

It can't be. I can't lose her. She is all that matters. Her, our son, my family. Where are they? Where am I?

This must be a dream. A nightmare. If I wake up, it will be over. I slap myself across the face. Pain explodes on my nose, my lips, blasting my thoughts into exploding stars. As my vision clears, I look around and... nothing.

An empty street in a dead city is all I see. I've lost them. Nothing else matters.

5

AMARA

"*W*here is he?" I ask myself for the hundredth time as I reach the wall again.

I stare out the window. The suns are low, creating long shadows stretching across the floor. He should have been home hours ago. I didn't worry for a while—he's been late before. No one can control everything out there, and sometimes it takes longer to unload the supplies, or there could have been a problem with the bivo. Now... now there's no more excuses. He should be home.

I pace across the room then back again. I run my fingers through my hair, scratching my head.

"He's okay, he's okay, he's okay," I mutter under my breath.

I can't let this bother me. If I show how scared I am, then Malcolm will get upset. More upset, I amend, looking at our son who's watching me while moving his stone figures around on the kitchen table.

He knows. I'm not stupid, and I know he's not either. He knows I'm worried and he knows his father should be home, but he's handling it better than I am. Malcolm is like that, always has been. If I were to look up the word resolute in a dictionary, then Malcolm's picture would be there.

Like we have dictionaries, but whatever. It's not the point. Malcolm takes most everything in stride. He's a child and his world is unshakable. Which is the way we want it. All the work that Shidan and I are doing, the Council, the bivo project, all of it is for him and all the kids. We're creating a future for them. One that will suck less than the one we have right now.

Well, mine doesn't suck. It's hard, sure, but I'm happy. I've never been happier than I've been since I gave in to Shidan.

God knows I didn't want to. I thought he was a creeper when we first met. I snort and shake my head remembering how I was back then. Wow. I was a total bitch. I can't believe he didn't give up on me.

He probably would have if the Zmaj weren't all about fated mates. I don't know about that, but I do know I love him. Isn't that enough?

Of course loving him isn't easy. Love never is, I suppose.

I love him so much I can't imagine life without him, for one. And that is why I'm pacing the floor, staring out the window, and barely keeping my shit under control. I clench my teeth, spin on my heel, and start across the room in the opposite direction again. And again. And again.

Damn it, Shidan, where are you?

Dark thoughts keep sliding in, and I do my best to push them away, but every time I make it across the room it becomes harder to resist. They come faster. And faster. And darker.

At first, he's hurt, but now, they're worse. What if he is... no. I'm not thinking that. He's fine. He got tied up, that's all. He'll come in that door any minute, and the moment he does, I'm going to kill him. Then I'm going to love him, and then I'm never letting him out that door again.

The suns drop lower still. It's almost night. The last rays of dusk stretch across the mostly empty space of our living room. That's it. I can't stay in here any longer doing nothing. It's time for action.

"Malcolm," I say. "Get a water container."

"How come, Mommy?" he asks as he drops out of the chair that's too big for him still and walks to the cabinet.

"We're going to go help your daddy," I say.

Malcolm stops, staring at the floor in front of his feet, his shoulders slumped.

"Okay," he says, then he moves again.

"Is something wrong, honey?" I ask.

"No," Malcolm says, then pulling a waterskin out and going over to the tank of water we keep.

"You're sure?" I ask, walking over and kneeling next to him as he fills the skin.

"Yes, Mommy," he says, but he's not looking at me.

I touch his shoulder and he turns his head to look. He's frowning, and there's worry in his eyes.

"What is it?" I ask.

He shakes his head, then drops his eyes to the floor.

"I don't know, Mommy," he says. "It's something, but I don't know what, yet."

"You're worried, baby," I say, pulling him into a tight embrace. I rub his back as I crush him to my chest. "It's fine. I'm scared too."

"You are?" he asks.

"Sure," I say. "Even mommies and daddies get scared, Malcolm. You know what the secret to handling fear is?"

"No."

"You do something about it," I say, setting him back down. "Instead of sitting around worrying and being scared, figure out something you can do about that fear. Then get into action. That's what we're going to do. Okay?"

"Yes!" he says, brightening.

"Good. You and me, kiddo," I say tousling his hair. "We're going to go help your daddy."

"Yay!" he says, returning his attention to the waterskin.

Once we have water for the two of us, I grab the shock-stick from a shelf, and we head out. The shock-stick doesn't have any charge left in it but the weight of it in my hand feels right. We're going to be in the City, and in theory it's as safe as can be, but I don't run on theories. We're talking about the safety of my son.

Outside it's hotter, as usual. The streets are empty. It's so oddly quiet. Strange how you get used to a certain level of background noise. It's never been the level I was used to on the generation ship from before the crash, but it was there. On the ship there was the constant white-noise of the engines, creaking of the steel exterior, and the buzz of people. The City background noise has always been one of working and the soft hum of conversations.

Now it's too quiet. Creepily so.

I take Malcolm's hand. He's unusually somber too. Normally when we go outside, he's a bundling ball of energy, and it's all I can do to keep him halfway under control. He'll run ahead leaping up onto the walls and then gliding to the far side of the street. Anything he can do to imitate Illadon.

Now there's a handful! Calista must pull her hair out trying to channel that boy's energy. It drives me nuts handling Malcolm after he's been around Illadon, I can't imagine having to handle *him*.

"Which way, Mommy?" Malcolm asks.

"Let's go towards the bivo pens," I say.

"Good idea," he agrees.

We walk together quietly. My shoulders are tense, and a headache is forming. I roll my shoulders trying to ease the tension, but it returns as fast as it goes. I'm trying to look everywhere at the same time in case he's somewhere along our route. The suns drop lower and lower as we walk, but nothing. Not a sign of him.

The airlock comes into view ahead. We keep moving until we're in shouting distance of the guard. It's a guy I know there. He used to be a pilot, like me. He's an asshole, or he was. I haven't talked to him much since the crash. Weird, there's not that many of us survivors, yet I've managed not to see this guy in what, a year?

"Draker," I call out.

It would have to be him, wouldn't it? Of all the men on the ship who survived the crash and made it here, it would be the one I had the biggest rivalry with.

"Ow, Mommy," Malcolm yelps, and only now do I realize I've tightened my grip on his hand.

"Sorry, baby," I say softly.

Draker looks up, pushing off the stool he's sitting on while doing guard duty at the door. He looks down the street, staring into the dim light until I see recognition dawn on his face.

"I'll be damned," he says. "Stancher?"

"Yeah," I say. "Long time, no see."

"Long time is right," he says. "Been what, a year?"

"Probably," I say. "You know, time flies when you're having fun."

"Time flies when *you're* having fun," he counters. "Heard you made it right on to the Lady General's private Council. You ain't changed a bit, have you?"

Gritting my teeth, I let his insults pass. He hasn't changed a bit.

"Have you seen Shidan?" I ask.

"Shi-who?" he asks.

"Shi-dan," I say. "Zmaj, about this tall?"

"Oh you mean Shit-zon," he says, and follows up with a mean snicker.

"This guy is not nice," Malcolm says.

"No, honey, he's not," I say under my breath. "Right, have you seen him?"

He's trying to provoke me the same as he used to do on the ship. I'm not going to play into his mind games. I've walked that road and it doesn't go anywhere useful.

"Not for hours," he says. "He unloaded the delivery and tended to those overgrown, hairy-ass cows we're tending out there, then came through here after. He did seem a bit confused, but who knows with his kind."

"He seemed confused?" I ask.

This ass was probably a Gershom supporter. He's that kind of jerk and obviously more than a bit racist, or xenophobic since we're talking about hating aliens. Probably a better term for it. Or, in simplest terms, he's an asshole. I pull Malcolm closer to my side.

"Right, didn't seem right in the head," he says, running his hand over his close shaved hair.

My stomach is a hard knot and cold creeps out from my core and across my limbs.

"Which way did he go?" I ask, struggling to keep my voice calm.

Malcolm grips my leg tight. Draker grins and shakes his head.

"That way," he says pointing his finger behind me.

"Did you see if he turned off?" I ask.

"What do I look like, the Zmaj police?"

"Draker," I say, throat so tight it makes my voice sound like a growl.

Draker holds his hands up in front of himself and shakes his head. "Hey Stancher, keep it cool. No need for your hot-headed tactics. I wasn't really watching, but I think he might have turned off to the left about three blocks down."

"Thanks," I say, turning away.

"You know," he says. "He's not too bad of a guy, for an alien. You could do worse."

I narrow my eyes at him and try to figure out his game. He smiles and it looks genuine.

"Nothing more," he says, sitting back on the stool. "The old days are gone. This is our world, and you always did need a strong man to tame that wild streak."

"I'll take that as a compliment," I say.

"Good, it was meant as one," he says.

Shaking my head, I turn and walk in the direction he indicated. People can change, some at least. The old Draker never would have even given me that much niceness. He's still an asshole, but that's who he is.

"We'll find him, Mommy," Malcolm says.

"Right, baby," I agree, though I'm not really paying attention to him.

I'm trying to pay attention to every detail around us. Peering into the shadowy confines of the broken remains of buildings that might be hiding Shidan. This area was hit hard by whatever happened to the City before the Devastation. That combined with the intervening years has made this section of town worse off than most.

It looks like a bomb went off, but years ago. The structural beams of the buildings are twisted, some of them look partially melted, and the facades are blasted through with massive holes in them. Where there was once glass-like fronts, there is nothing.

If Shidan is in one of these, hurt or passed out, it will be impossible to find him. My chest clenches tight, and I have to push that thought aside. Something happened to him. That much is clear, the question is what?

Was there an accident? Did he get in a fight? With who? or what? Or is it worse... is he infected?

"Shidan!" I yell

"Daddy!" Malcolm yells helping with the search for his father.

Our own voices echo back to us mockingly. The City is huge, and the two of us alone are never going to find Shidan except by blind luck. I could go to Rosalind, ask her to help organize a search for him.

I could, except we're in lockdown. Quarantine because of an unseen, silent killer that is spreading through the Zmaj males. Addison's fear is it will mutate and affect the humans too. There won't be any help. We're on our own.

My hands tremor and I chew my lip, struggling to hold back tears. I yell for him again and nothing. He's hurt. He needs me. Needs us.

How do I find him?

"AMARA!"

Shidan! It's him, I heard his voice. I look down at Malcolm to make sure I'm not losing it, and the grin on his face tells me it was real. I scoop him up into my arms and run, seating him onto my hip as I go.

"That way, Mommy," Malcolm says, pointing.

He's heavy, and running with him on my hip is awkward, throwing my gait off, but I push on. Malcolm yells for his dad over and over. One block, two, and three. Nothing.

"Amara!" Shidan's voice echoes.

I can't tell which direction he is. It's almost full dark, the moons aren't out tonight, and it's making it even harder to figure out which direction to go to find him.

"That way, Mommy," Malcolm says pointing.

"Are you sure, baby?" I ask, and he nods emphatically.

"Okay," I say.

It doesn't seem right, but I'm not sure one way or the other. I've found before when Malcolm is certain of something, he's usually right. It's one of the 'unusual' aspects of our son. So I listen and run.

My lungs burn, and I'm heaving, when I turn a corner and see Shidan. Malcolm slides off my hip and runs to his dad. I run too, ignoring the need for air. Shidan jerks around at the sound of our approach. His tail rises behind his wings and his hands ball into fists. He's in a fighting position until he sees Malcolm running at him.

"Malcolm!" Shidan yells, opening his arms wide.

Malcolm leaps into the air feet away from his father and glides into his arms. Shidan pulls him in and holds him against his chest. I finish running up and something in Shidan's eyes is off. A cold pit full of ice forms in the pit of my stomach.

"Amara… my treasure," Shidan says, throwing one arm out and inviting me in.

I step into the comfort of his embrace. The scent of him fills my nostrils, and endorphins release, leaving me giddy with relief. I cling to him, unable to speak. Tears stream down my face, so I bury myself into his shoulder.

None of us speak, holding tight to each other until the emotions overwhelming us pass. When the tears slow, and my breath stops hitching, I wipe my cheeks with both hands and run my hands through my hair.

"Are you all right?" I ask, stepping back so I can look at him.

It's hard to see in the dark, but I can't see anything physically wrong.

"I'm fine," he says. "I missed you both."

"Why didn't you come home?" I ask, frowning.

His forehead wrinkles and his eyes dart around. He opens his mouth then snaps it shut.

"I was…" he says trailing off.

"And? What happened? Draker says you seemed confused when you came through the airlock."

"The airlock," he says, shaking his head. "Right…"

"Daddy, what's wrong?" Malcolm asks.

"Nothing, son," he says and smiles. "Daddy is fine. We should get home."

The cold pit in my stomach drops to the ground. The look on his face is clear. He doesn't know the way home. He was lost. Bile rises in my throat, so I swallow hard.

"Good idea," I say, forcing my voice to remain calm. "Let's get home. It's past dinnertime."

Shidan nods his agreement.

"I'm hungry," Malcolm says.

"Of course you are," I say. "You're a growing boy."

I take Shidan's hand and lead him toward home. The fears assailing my thoughts are a storm of dark wings, but I can't let on to it in front of Malcolm. I don't want him to know how bad it is. Worse, I don't know how bad it's going to be.

6

SHIDAN

"*H*e's infected," the human female in the white coat says.

She's talking to Amara, and I don't know if she doesn't think I can hear her, or what. I'm right here, why is she not talking to me?

Something about this female seems familiar, but I don't think I know her. She reminds me of someone I once knew though. That's what it is. She's similar to someone I used to know. Since she's not talking to me, I pass the time studying the room.

It's a nice space. Better than the cave I was living in. I've done well for...

I look at the female that says she's my mate. I know her name. Her name is... Amara. Treasure. The way my hearts quicken, and my breath catches when I look at her, I know she's the one. My dragon chose her, but when? I can't recall. It stirs though, recognizing her, claiming her.

"Oh," Amara says.

BANG! BANG!

I leap from the bed I was on and land, placing myself

between Amara and the unknown source of the noise. Something is hitting something. I hold her behind me with one arm while I look for the trouble.

"It's fine," the white-coated female is yelling to be heard over the ongoing noise.

I bare my teeth and clench my free hand into a fist, backing away from the noise, pushing Amara behind me. There's a soft roar, muffled but definite. This situation is far from fine. Growling under my breath I look for the source of the sound. It's coming from the far side of the wall.

Amara places a hand on my bicep, pulling my attention to her. She smiles, shakes her head.

"It's okay, Shidan," she says. "It's Ladon, nothing more."

Ladon? A male's name. Some male is threatening my mate? My wings rustle and my tail vibrates, ready for combat. I turn back towards the sound and stride across the room, raising my hands, ready to fight.

"Shidan, no!" the white-coated female yells.

I glance over my shoulder and bare my teeth to silence her. No male will threaten my female. Amara runs to my side, grabbing my arm and pulling until I stop and turn to face her.

"No," she says. "Shidan, no. It's fine, he's not threatening me."

The banging stops. I stare at the door that blocks me from seeing the source. Amara says its fine, and I trust her, so I relax.

"Come, sit down, please," white-coated female says.

I follow them back to the bed and take a seat on its edge, but I'm watching the door. Nothing will come in and catch me unaware.

"Addison," Amara says. "What can I do? He's…"

She trails off looking at me. Moisture glistens in the corners of her eyes. I recognize this, there is a term for it. I know it, it's… the fog in my head surges. The word is right there, on the tip of my tongue, but… nothing. I don't recall it.

It's bad, though. A human thing? Yes, a human reaction. Zmaj do not waste water like that. I reach out and wipe a droplet of the moisture from her cheek. A faltering smile dances across her lips. I cup my hand around the back of her head and pull her against my shoulder, holding her.

The white-coated woman watches, silent, but worry lines her face. She's frowning and concerned. That feeling that I know her name, that I know this female flits through my head, but I can't nail it. She is one I do know, I recognize her, but then I don't know her at the same time.

An empty tingling sensation itches inside my head. It's annoying, frustrating. I want to reach into my own skull and scratch it, but that, of course, is impossible. The more it builds, behind it is a deeper sensation. A coldness in the pit of my stomach.

I don't understand it, and that makes me angry. I want to smash something, destroy whatever is causing my female to shed moisture. I have no target.

"I wish I knew," the white-coat woman says, her voice barely a whisper. She clears her throat and rubs her eyes with the heels of her hands. Shaking her head, she straightens and drops her hands to her side. "I have a couple of ideas though."

"What?" Amara asks, pulling out of my embrace and giving the other female her attention.

"The shipwreck is first," she says. "There might still be equipment there we haven't salvaged. Or supplies, drugs maybe. I need better scanners, though I'm not sure we'd have the resources to power them. The machines I have won't give me a clear picture of what's happening in the Zmaj head. I need to see how this virus is affecting their brains."

"Fine," Amara says. "I'll go and get it. Do you know what it looks like?"

"You can't go alone," she says.

"I won't be," Amara says. "Shidan will go with me."

"Amara," she purses her lips and hesitates before finishing her thought. "that's not a good idea."

"Why?" Amara asks, hands on her hips.

"He's going..." she trails off.

"Where am I going?" I ask.

The white-coated female looks at me and frowns. She inhales deeply then lets it out in a long sigh.

"You're going to get worse," she says. "The pattern so far is you'll continue to regress, getting worse and worse."

"Until?" Amara asks.

The female's eyes dart towards the door where the sound came from.

"Until he's gone," she says.

"Gone?" Amara asks.

"Primal. The man you know and love will be more animal than man," she sighs.

Silence is a heavy weight across all of us. It doesn't make sense. I'm fine, how can it be that I'm losing to... the bijass?

It takes me a moment to recall the word. Words are getting harder. Is this what she means? This must be a sign of what's happening. The disease. I was exposed.

"We'll go," I say, taking Amara's hand. "We'll find this equipment you need. You will find a cure."

Amara squeezes my hand tight and nods her agreement. The other female shrugs and nods.

"I don't have any choice," she says. "I need help, and Ormarr is lost to me too."

"Describe what you need," I say.

She launches into a description of the machines, and Amara makes careful notes for us. She also names off several words that make no sense to me, but Amara notes them as well. While the females discuss and throw about strange words, I study Amara.

Her jaw is strong, almost sharp, but comes down to a beautiful round chin. The way her brow wrinkles when she frowns. Her eyes alight with a fever, every motion of her body calling to be in action. She's fierce. A fire burns inside of her soul that calls my dragon. I can feel it stirring behind the fog over my thoughts.

Is the fog nothing more than the breath of the dragon? The smoke coming from its fiery breath as it burns away all that's unnecessary? Am I regressing as this female says, or am I progressing? Moving away from complexity towards simplicity and certainty?

When Amara finishes with her sketches and notes, the two females stare until I stop my musing and give them my attention.

"You need to fight it," the other female says. "Hang on to every memory. Ormarr has had some success. Ladon woke up without his memory but Ormarr has remained less... primal. It's the only advice I can give you."

"I fight well," I say.

"Of course you do, my love," Amara says. "We will beat this. I won't lose you."

"You are my treasure, nothing can ever take that from us," I say. "I will always love you."

Amara smiles but the water runs from her eyes as if it's being poured from a container. Beading down her cheeks and dripping off her chin. I pull her close and hold her tight.

"Get going," the other female says, wiping moisture from her own eyes. "There isn't time to waste."

"Can you get a message to Jolie?" Amara asks. "Tell her what's happening. She'll need to keep Malcolm safe for us."

My dragon roars inside and I growl. "No."

"No?" Amara asks, looking at me with wide eyes.

"No," I growl, jerking my hand from hers. "Malcolm. Our son. Stays."

Amara's eyes narrow and she shakes her head.

"Shidan, you're not thinking clearly," she says. "We are not taking him out into the desert with us."

The mind-fog swells, red comes across my vision. The dragon rumbling inside is loud making it harder and harder to think. Malcolm is mine. I protect him, no other. My child. My son. Mine to protect.

"No," I shake my head, but I'm not answering her, I'm struggling. Fighting for control of my own thoughts.

"Shidan," Amara says, placing her hands on my chest. "Please. He'll be safer here. It's enough for you to worry about me out there. We can't take our son with us."

Her words... make sense. I know it. They cut through the fog, appeal to the voice of reason that is being drowned in the swirling mists of primality engulfing me. No matter how right she is, the dragon doesn't want to accept it. He is mine, I must protect him. No other.

I growl, unable to contain it. My shoulders are tight knots. I force my body to relax, unknotting the tension in the muscles, taking my attention down from the shoulders through my torso, down my limbs. Push calm, cling to reason, bringing my thoughts under control.

Silently she runs her hands over my chest and up on to my face. She pulls my attention down to her. I stare into her eyes as she wraps her arms around me. In her I find my anchor. She is my treasure, my life, my sanity.

"Okay," I agree, defying the screaming instincts that tell me to trust no other.

"Good," she says, rising onto the balls of her feet she kisses me.

Her tongue pushes past my pliant lips as our kiss deepens. My arms wrap around her body, hands dropping to her full ass. My prime cock stiffens between us and I'm about to lift her up, fully ready to take what is mine when the other female clears her throat.

63

"Uh, I hate to interrupt but... not alone here?" she asks.

Amara's face turns a soft pink that only entices me more, but she breaks our embrace and straightens her clothing.

"Sorry," she says shaking her head.

I don't understand what she is sorry for, but I keep my silence. On some level I understand the humans don't express love this openly.

"You two need to move," the other female says. "I don't know how long you'll have."

"Right," Amara says, taking my hand. "We'll grab packs and go immediately."

She pulls me out of the room. We make our way out of the building where the medical facility is and emerge into the empty, dead City. The temperature goes up as we step out, and I tilt my head back, taking the moment to enjoy the warmth.

When I open my eyes and look around, the empty streets and the decaying buildings strike an analogy to what's happening in my head. The past is like this scene before me. Devoid of meaning and serving no purpose. My stomach knots at the thought, and a cold chill causes me to shiver.

"What is it?" Amara asks.

"Nothing," I say, shaking my head.

"That was more than nothing," she observes.

I can't tear my eyes away from the scene. She puts her arm around my waist and follows my gaze.

"It's empty, purposeless," I say.

"Yeah," she agrees. "The quarantine has really killed the buzz."

"It's how my head feels," I say, speaking softly, almost not saying it.

She gasps but doesn't say anything. Instead she squeezes me tighter and then her breath resumes.

"We need to go," she urges, moving.

I follow her because I don't know where she's going. I know

we are to get supplies. I should know where we would do that. I feel like I do know, but I don't have any clue of how to get there.

We make our way through several blocks of the city until we get to a building that she must recognize. I look at it and can't see how it stands out from any of the multitude we passed on our way here. There is nothing about it that stands out, but I put my trust in her.

Inside she pulls me along and through the interior until we're in a new apartment. Small stone figures litter the floor. I pick up two of them and look them over. They're crudely shaped stone, carved to resemble people and monsters. A child's toys.

"I could do better than this," I mutter, staring at a figure that looks like it was meant to be a zemlja.

Amara stops what she was doing and stares as if I've said something wrong. I look up from the figure in my hand.

"What?" I ask.

"You did make those," she says softly.

"Oh," I say, staring at the toy again.

Nothing. I don't recognize it. Yet I made it?

An empty ache pulses in my head and is mirrored in my stomach. I drop the toy and rise to my feet. I walk over to Amara, who is holding a bag that she is filling with basic supplies. Dried meats and such. I see a waterskin sitting on the counter, so I pick it up then look around for a place to fill it.

There's a tank sitting behind me, so I fill the skin there. When it's done, I sling it over my shoulder and look to see if she is ready. She has the bag in her hand, so I take that and sling it across my opposite shoulder, adjusting the two bags so they won't interfere with access to my lochaber.

"Ready?" I ask and she nods. "Then lead the way, my treasure. Please."

I see it in her eyes. She knows I'm asking her to lead

because I don't know how to get there. The reproach in her look tells me I should and that she isn't fooled by my coverup. My chest tightens, but there is nothing I can do about it.

She leads us out of the building and through the empty streets. Our echoing footsteps are the only sound until we're close to the dome. A male sits on a stool next to the airlock. He rises to his feet when he sees us approaching.

"See you found him," the male says.

The scales on back of my neck itch. I don't like this male. Something about him puts me on edge. I want to keep him away from Amara.

"Yes," Amara says, her shoulders squaring, jaw clenching, and her hands balling into fists. "Thank you."

She doesn't slow her stride, so I keep pace with her as we close the distance.

"Woah," the male says. "No one is supposed to go outside. Lockdown, don't you know? Besides, you already lost him once, you want to lose him outside there? Whole damn planet he could get lost in."

"Out of the way, Draker," Amara growls. "Stay back and keep the distancing in, right?"

He backs away holding his hands up and making a patting motion.

"Sure," he says. "Trying to be helpful. No need to take it all wrong now."

"I'm not," Amara says, working the panel to the airlock. "We're in a hurry."

"Hurry for what?" the male asks.

"If she wanted to tell you, she would have," I say through clenched teeth.

The itching in my head, the rising red, I want nothing more than an excuse to hurt this male. His attitude challenges my dominance. The dragon will not be challenged. I am the dominant here, and there is nothing I want more than to show him.

Only a thin thread of rationality keeps me from putting him in his place.

"Okay, see we're grumpy," the male says.

The door whooshes open.

"Come on," Amara says.

I follow her into the airlock and watch as the door closes behind us. An urge to run swells, to get free of the small space, but I control it. It's silly and unnecessary. Amara is calm, I'll be calm too.

The male returns to his seat and grins through the transparent door portions of the airlock at us. I growl, my tail rising between my shoulders. Amara puts a hand on my shoulder.

"Trust me," she says. "He isn't worth it."

The air pressure shifts, and the door out opens. We walk through and the full force of the two suns of Tajss hit us. I spread my arms, close my eyes, and lean my head back, enjoying it. I spread my wings and bask in the glorious warmth. It feels good, natural, like coming home.

"You would enjoy it," Amara grumps.

"Do you not?" I ask, looking at her.

Moisture beads the line of her hair at the top of her face and her skin has taken on a reddish hue. Something tickles my thoughts, a memory, I try to grasp it, wrestling it from the fog. She doesn't like the heat. Then it hits me.

"Epis!" I yell, surprised by my own thought coming through clear.

"What about it?" she asks.

"You brought epis? You'll need it."

"I brought some," she says nodding towards the pack I carry. "Our supplies are low in the City. I don't need it as often as I used to though, should be okay. One advantage of long-term taking of it. It stays in my system longer, or something."

"Good," I say.

She smiles and my hearts soar. This is what matters. Her smile is brighter than both the suns above.

"This way," she says, pointing and walking.

The suns are not high in the sky as we set off on our journey. We don't make it far before I hook an arm around her to help her travel. She sinks into the sand and has a difficult time walking. I use my wings to make us lighter, but it's still slow going.

She doesn't complain, stoically making progress, but the suns are reaching their mid-point and we've not traveled far at all. On a whim, I hook an arm behind her knees and sweep her up to carry her. Now I run.

Wings wide I run, puffs of sand exploding from each placement of my feet. As the warm breeze grows stronger, I leap into it, and we glide for many strides before landing. I make a short run then repeat the process.

I laugh. It feels so good to be in motion, I can't contain my pleasure. Her in my arms, running across the open sands, nothing could be more perfect. She points every so often, and I adjust our course to keep it in line with where she directs. We travel in this fashion until the suns are setting, and we haven't reached our destination.

I come to a stop and let her slide down back onto her own feet. She shields her eyes and stares out at the horizon, grimacing.

"It's going to be tomorrow," she says. "No way we can make it tonight."

"I can keep going," I offer.

She turns back and smiles. "Of course you can. Is it wise though?"

I think about her words. Is it wise? I shrug, uncertain of an actual answer to give her.

"I do not know," I admit.

"You have always told me traveling at night isn't wise," she says.

"I have?" I ask.

It doesn't sound like anything I would say. I can run all night, so let's run. Was I doubting my own fitness?

"Yes, my love," she says, her hand running down my arm. "We should find shelter or make a small fire."

"Yes, a fire," I say. "It keeps the flier at bay."

"Sismis," she says.

Frowning I nod agreement that I don't feel. The word she said means nothing to me. Perhaps it is a human term. It doesn't matter, I must prepare a fire.

"There is no wood," I say looking around.

"In the bag," she says indicating the pack I took from her before we left.

I slip it off and open up, going through the contents. There is a small supply of sticks and some dried dung to burn. It's all I need to build a serviceable fire. Once I have all the pieces in place, I get close and belch a flame to get it started. It takes me two attempts, but then I have it going. She gets out some pieces of dried meat, and we cuddle up close to the fire.

The suns are below the horizon, and I'm not running, so the chill of the night is seeping in. She is a welcome warmth to my cold scales. I throw one leg over the top of her and we eat in a comfortable silence, holding on to each other.

I can't imagine a better life. My treasure in my arms, a fire, food in our bellies. This is what a male is. A protector and a provider. Nothing dares disturb our peace, knowing full well I am the superior predator. Her head nods and she jerks it back.

"Sleep my treasure, do not fight it, I have you," I say, patting her beautiful rear.

"You sure?" she asks, yawning.

"Of course," I say. "Here, use my shoulder for your head."

I shift so that my shoulder will be a better pillow for her to sleep on and she adjusts. In moments she is asleep, her breathing becoming regular. I watch her chest rise and fall for a while then put my attention out past the small fire.

The desert stretches on for as far as I can see. Home is out there. I recall home. A nice cave where my woman would be safe while I hunt. I don't recall her there though. The dim memories of home I have are empty. No female, no Amara. Was I alone there?

I could go though, but something about the City calls me back. I pull at the strings of the thought until it comes back.

Malcolm.

My hearts race and pain strikes hard into my chest. I tighten my arm around Amara pulling her closer. She murmurs in her sleep but doesn't wake up.

How?

Now, for the first time, I feel something is wrong. Forgetting my son?

My thoughts spin out of control. I forgot my son? Anger wars with terror leaving my arms trembling as I struggle to remain in control of my own mind. Forgetting everything else I can justify. It's fine, I don't need to remember the names of random humans or others.

Forget Amara? Forget Malcolm?

I would have thought it impossible. How could a male forget his own child?

Cold stretches through my limbs paralyzing me. It leaves no room for doubt. I've contracted the virus.

I'm sick and if we don't find a cure, I could lose everything.

7

AMARA

I wake up stiff and sore. As I stretch, Shidan shifts and gives me room.

"Mmm, morning," I murmur, barely opening my eyes.

"Yes, my treasure," he says softly.

I roll my shoulders then my head as I sit up. Multiple bones crack and crackle as I move.

"God, I hate sleeping in the desert," I say.

"Do you?" he asks.

The utter curiosity in his voice and on his face makes my stomach drop. He knows this. It's not like we have secrets between us. He's forgetting more.

"Yeah," I say, smiling and trying to cover over the fear making my chest hurt and my stomach feel like a hard ball of ice. "We should get going."

"You need to eat," he says, rising up and going to the pack.

The small fire has burned down to ash and to be sure I'm not hungry. Watching the man I love lose his mind isn't appetite inducing. He ignores me though, pulling out some of the carefully wrapped foods.

"I'll eat as we go," I say.

He's losing it fast if he got this much worse overnight. I don't know how long we have but it's obviously not enough. We need to find a cure now. Addison told me in private she's worried that the damage to their brains could be permanent. That if it goes too far the infected Zmaj might never recover, never get their memories back.

"Are you sure?" he asks, looking over his shoulder

"Yes," I say, walking over and gathering up the things that lie scattered outside the pack.

I don't want to waste a minute. Not on eating, not on packing, nothing. If it wasn't on the edge of suicidal to travel without supplies I'd leave it all behind to get moving now.

He won't be swayed from his insistence on feeding me though. He unwraps the meat, moving in what looks like slow freaking motion, and pulls out three pieces. He hands two to me and pops one in his mouth.

Finally he replaces the wrapping and by the time I've packed everything else that was removed from the pack he's put the meat back in. I've also finished my first piece of meat and put the second into my mouth by this time.

He slings the pack over his shoulder and then scoops me up. I indicate the direction we need to go, and he nods as if he knew it already, but I know he's covering. I can see it in his eyes. I know him too well. He can't hide the fact that he's lost out here.

"Run, my love," I whisper in his ear. "Please run."

He doesn't answer with words but with actions. I don't know if he's afraid or responding to my own unspoken fear, but he runs and runs fast. It's almost as if we're flying across the desert. Each leap he takes we go for a dozen yards, and he barely touches down before he's leaping forward again.

We make great time across the desert. The suns aren't fully above the horizon when the wreck of the generation ship appears and dominates the horizon.

Seeing the wreck again stirs old emotions I haven't looked at in years. The sheer size of the thing is crazy. It's bigger than any building in the City. It's bigger than any dozen buildings together in the City.

It makes me feel small and brings back all the old memories. That life, who I was, none of that is me any longer. I was angry. Fighting everything and everyone. It's who I was when we crashed here, but all of that was before. Before Shidan and before Malcolm.

The structure of the ship is like a massive skyscraper rising up like a gray-black finger trying to scrape the suns above it. I don't know and can't imagine how many people lived on the ship, and this is only a section of it.

Did other sections survive the crash? Are there other survivors out there?

It could be. Annabel and her group are a perfect example of it. We've been so busy surviving, trying to make a home for ourselves and adjust to our new lives, I haven't given the idea much thought. Rosalind probably has though. It's the kind of thing Rosalind thinks about.

"That is our goal?" Shidan asks.

My heart skips a beat. He doesn't know.

"Yes," I say, touching his cheek.

His eyes dart down, and I see clearly, he has no recollection of the ship. Behind my eyelids, tears threaten, but I hold them at bay. The extreme heat helps. Even with epis and regularly sipping the water, I'm on the edge of dehydration. Yay for that.

He nods and runs faster, then leaps. The warm breeze blasts away the last threat of tears as we glide. I close my eyes to protect them from the bits of grit in the wind, turning my face into his chest. He won't be able to miss the landmark of the wreck, so I'll let him get us there.

It frees me to let my mind wander through the past. After we crashed, I hated the way Shidan followed me. Every time I'd turn around, there he was. I swear I bumped into him more times than I can count. He was like a ninja, appearing out of nowhere at the most unexpected and often the most inopportune moments.

I was a bitch. Let's be honest about it. I treated him like shit, and the fact that he saw through all my issues and still was able to love me is a testament to the man he is. Now... now I'm scared I'm going to lose him.

What if he forgets me? Forgets our son? How do I bring him back to us? Can I?

I tighten my grip around his neck and desperately struggle not to bawl. The idea of it is overwhelming. I can't even begin to handle him not being here, not being him. The way he plays with Malcolm.

It reminds me when I found out I was pregnant. I handled it the same way I handle most things. Lashing out at all the wrong targets. Wow, have I not gotten any better over the years? Shidan though, his excitement was a fountain of overwhelming joy. I couldn't stay angry around him. Probably because I wasn't angry. I was scared. I'd seen what Calista and Jolie had to go through to have their kids. It was terrifying. Fear. I don't know how to deal with fear.

When I was a space jockey flying fighter ships, fear didn't exist. I had this simplistic view of the world that kept it at bay. I knew, back then, I was going to die young. I wasn't living for a future, I was living for the moment.

All that mattered was that I was the best. If I couldn't be the best, if I couldn't prove I belonged in the old boys' club, then I'd rather have been dead. I would die pushing the limits of what could be done, but I'd have done it.

I was an idiot.

Now I know what's important, and it's not about me. It's about him. About Malcolm. It's really about the future world Shidan and I are creating with our friends for our kids. It's still about what we do, but dying young would be pointless, wouldn't it? There's so much to do.

I've barely kept enough power working in the City to run the dome. I've accomplished nothing on getting any form of reliable power to the apartments. We only recently got fresh water that is drinkable, but it's only in one location, and everyone has to go there to take some.

It's not enough. My dreams are so much bigger. I want to create a world that when Shidan and I do die, hopefully in each other's arms, we can be proud of what we leave for Malcolm.

I want to see Malcolm grow up, become a man, find a mate of his own. Give his heart to another. I want grandchildren! I want everything that any mother wants. And I want Shidan by my side for all of it. Doing this alone? That's a darkness I don't think I can make my way through. It makes my insides cold and freezes my thoughts. I shy away from it.

That is what I'm afraid of, losing him. Losing what we have together. I cling to him as if by strength of arm alone I can keep him with me. Keep him from slipping away and losing his memories of us. Tighter and tighter until the shadow of the shipwreck falls over us and we've arrived.

Shidan comes to a halt and lowers me to the ground. I lean against him and we stare up at the wreckage of the lives that were. So many lives were lost in this wreck that they are innumerable. I don't think any of us can comprehend the number. We don't talk about it and I, for one, avoid thinking about it. Partly because I know, deep in my heart, it was my fault. I was a fighter pilot. My entire job was to protect the ship in case we ran into any unfriendly types.

We didn't launch a single fighter. The entire attack was done by surprise, and that still doesn't sit well with me. How did we not know an attack was coming? The ship was equipped with redundant systems to warn us—but nothing? It's not possible.

Or it shouldn't be, but here I am looking at the irrefutable evidence that it is.

"Are you okay?" Shidan asks.

"Yeah," I say, shaking my head to clear it of unanswered questions. "We should get in there."

He nods and wraps his arm around my waist. Together we close the last distance to the wreck. As we draw closer, the wear and tear of exposed metal in the desert becomes obvious. Holes are being worn through the steel of the ship exterior. The constant blasting sand doing its slow work of eroding the metal.

There are enough holes now that I wonder how many years it will be before the remains of the ship collapses on itself. That's going to make it a challenge to explore the inside. I hope the interior structure isn't too compromised.

"Do you think creatures have taken up a home in it?" I ask.

"It would make sense," he says. "What is this?"

I look up, unsure what he's asking about, but he's staring up at the wreck itself. There's a blankness to his expression.

"This is part of the generation ship that all of us humans were on. It crashed here?"

"Oh," he says, and shakes his head slightly.

"You don't know this?" I ask, pressing the point.

He purses his lips and furrows his brow, then at last he shakes his head. "No, I don't."

"Oh," I say, the pit in my stomach roiling with acid. "What do you recall?"

I'm scared to ask, but I do it anyway.

"A sign," he says, frowning. "A calling. I had to answer it. I knew... you were waiting for me."

I smile, warmed by his words which ease the depths of my concern.

"Okay," I say. "We should be able to climb in over here."

I lead the way around base of the wreck until we come to

the opening. The opening is where this section of the ship was torn off the rest of it by the forces of gravity as we crashed to Tajss. A cold tingle races down my limbs.

My memories of that night are vivid flashes. Frozen moments in time, but pieces of it are missing. Emerging from my bunk to a smoke-filled corridor with the alarms blaring and flashing red lights. Racing to get to the flight deck. Fighting what I now know to call Zzlo.

The rumbling. I'll never forget that rumbling sound as something exploded deep in the ship. I knew, right then, that we were doomed. In that moment I kissed my ass goodbye and sent out my last prayers.

Little did I know, those prayers would be answered. I was never much of a believer, but in a moment like that, I think everyone becomes a believer in something. You have to. It's the only way to deal with what's happening to you. That sense of being absolutely out of control of your own fate.

The next thing I recall is seeing the tear in the deck. Then I blacked out. When I woke up, everything hurt. And we were here. On this godforsaken desert hellhole. Home. A world I wouldn't change for all the universe, now. Back then I'd have traded it for anything.

The warm breeze rustles the sheets of plastic that we'd used to create a sense of safety, though now it's mostly torn or rotted away. Remnants of it hang from the broken trusses high over our heads. A handful of crates, mostly buried in sand, dot the interior. I'm sure they're empty remnants, already raided for salvage. Our job today isn't going to be that easy.

"Where will we find the machine?" Shidan asks.

"Up there," I say, pointing above us and biting my lip.

He should know this. He does know this. Except he doesn't.

Shidan stares up then looks around the area. Silently, he sets to work, grabbing the remaining crates and salvage and stacking it to form a ladder up. I help, though some of them are too big and heavy for me to even attempt to lift. We work together until there's a serviceable ladder ready for us to use.

"You go first," Shidan says. "That way, I can catch you if you fall."

Nodding my agreement, I start the climb. It's treacherous. The makeshift ladder shifts under my weight, sliding and scraping. More than once, my stomach drops as I think I'm about to fall, but somehow, I manage to steady myself and continue climbing.

I'm over halfway up when Shidan starts climbing too. His greater weight causes the crates to shift down, and I yelp. He puts a hand on my back, steadying me, then we continue. If I stretch my arm all the way up, I can get my fingers over the lip of the door I'm trying to reach.

"Can you push me up?" I ask.

"Yes," Shidan says, He puts his hand on my ass and boosts me up.

He lifts me up a foot with no effort. I get both hands over the lip of the open doorway and then pull myself up and over. I slide across the lip to stand on what was once the wall. A few moments later, Shidan leaps up into the opening, wings open, and he lands balanced on that same lip, then moves to the opposite side. He grins, and in that shining moment, I see my man. The joy and delight he lives his life with, taking so much pleasure in the simplest of things. That's my Shidan.

Sure, the very thing that used to drive me nuts is the thing I figured out I love most about him, but isn't that true of most things? He has a youthful outlook. Life is meant to be enjoyed, and he makes the most of every moment.

"Where to now?" he asks.

"Well, the medical area is that way," I say. "It's where we'll need to go, I think."

Don't think about it, Amara. Push the worry aside. It doesn't matter he should remember all this. It's the past, who remembers the past anyway? Nothing there but old bones and worries. He's going to be fine.

Together we work our way up to the former medical bay. It's hard, exhausting work. Luckily, so far, we haven't found any signs of life except for droppings that stain what was the decks. I'm purposefully not thinking about what left the dung. I'm fine to get in and get out without any excitement, thank you very much.

When we finally climb through the last opening it's as much of a mess as I remember it being. Worse thanks to decay and other raiders hitting it up. The march of time has taken a heavy toll. The outer wall, which was once the floor, has holes worn through it giving glimpses of the darkening sky outside. That also allowed sand in.

Sand is everywhere, carried by the constant breeze that makes its way across Tajss. Sometimes that breeze is a full-on gale-force wind, in which case the sand becomes a blasting, destroying power. The dome over the City protects us from the worst effects of that now, but the ship has no such protection.

The machines were already bashed around in the crash and now they're filled with sand. As I work my way through the piles with Shidan's help, my hope weakens. I don't think we're going to find anything working here. The dim light coming through the holes fades until we're working in heavy dusk.

I grab another crate, intending to toss it to one side, then something flashes beneath it, darting towards me. Shidan growls and moves faster than the thing coming at me, grabbing it out of midair. My heart pounds and my head hurts as I look at the thing in his hand.

It's a snake, or close enough to be considered one. It writhes in his hand, its small head trying to curl around to bite him. He grabs it with his other hand and rips it in half, then tosses it aside. I swallow hard and do my best to not break down into a quivering mess.

"Very dangerous," he says. "Poison."

"Right." I take a deep breath and let it out slowly.

Sometimes the planet likes to give us a reminder that our environment is dangerous. Especially when it seems like it's the least dangerous.

We work together until I'm exhausted. As I try to lift yet another crate my muscles tremble and refuse to pick it up. I drop to the floor and lean back against the wall, huffing and puffing. Shidan lifts the crate I was attempting to and sets it over in the done pile, the ones we've explored. After he finishes, he comes and sits down next to me.

"This is hopeless," I say.

He rests his hand on my knee but doesn't say a word. He's staring off into the darkness that's claiming the medical bay. Already it's to the point I can't really see, but I know his eyesight is much better than my own in these situations.

"What are we looking for?" he asks after a while.

I stare at him as my stomach drops. My chest tightens and my throat constricts. I can't form the words for some time. He turns and looks, waiting for my answer. I shake my head, biting my lip to try and hold back the tears. He smiles but his eyes are empty of understanding. He truly doesn't remember why we came here.

"We're looking for a machine," I remind him.

"Oh," he says, not showing any sign of the deeper understanding I want him to have. That I desperately need him to have.

"You're sick," I say. "Remember?"

"I'm sick?" he asks, surprise in his voice and on his face when he looks back to me.

"Oh, Shidan," I say, unable to hold back my tears any longer.

I touch his face, tracing the lines I know like the back of my hand. He leans into my touch, replicating it by touching my face too.

"You are very beautiful," he says softly.

"Thank you," I say through my tears.

"Why are you sad? I want to fix it," he says.

My tears choke me, and I can't answer. I shake my head and scoot over until I'm in his lap and resting my head on his chest. I'm losing him, and there's not a damn thing I can do about it.

8

SHIDAN

*T*he fog in my head grows thicker and thicker. While we were working, I didn't notice but when we stopped to rest, and I wanted to ask her about what we're doing I realize what's happening. She rests curled up in my lap. I run my hands through her hair, down her back, and then back up.

She doesn't speak, and I'm grateful for it. My words have hurt her, and that's the last thing I want. I know I'm sick, but I don't feel like I am. If anything, I feel fine, if not for the thick feeling in my head. It's a little hard to think, but I don't need to think to know I love her.

Holding her in my arms is right. I know it. The dragon stirs in my core breathing its fire. That fire burns through my veins. She is mine. My treasure. We belong together.

She sobs and the sound of it breaks my heart. I don't understand her sadness. I am here, we are together, and I will destroy anything that tries to harm her. Formless anger surges bringing the cloud of instinct with it, but I push that down. There is no enemy here to face.

"Shhh," I say, a soothing sound. "What is wrong, my treasure? I would destroy that which bothers you."

She sobs harder, shoulder shaking as she grabs me tighter and buries her face against my chest. I don't know how to help so I hold her and wait. Eventually I hope it will be clear what I should do. Nothing does come clear, but soon her breathing evens out, and then she is asleep.

I hold her tight, refusing to move even as my muscles burn from being locked into one place for too long. I'm not going to disturb her rest. She must need it. I look around the room we're in. We came here for something, though I don't remember what.

I think I should remember. It seems I know it, but what it is won't come to mind. So I contemplate that, trying to remember what it was we were hoping to find here. This is the... ship. Yes, she called it a ship.

It was the transport that her race was on. It's fall from the sky to Tajss created the sign I followed. The sign that called telling me to find her. She is from the skies, so that makes her an angel. My angel.

Moonlight creeps its way across the sky until it's falling through the rotting holes in the ceiling above us, casting the space in a silvery hue. Something is making my scales itch on the back of my neck, and I know something is wrong. What it is, I don't know, but something.

Senses on high alert, I study the shadows, watching for any threat. There, to the left, something moves. Darting from one shadow to another. Little more than a splotch of darkness itself, but the motion does not escape my attention.

Staring into the shadow's last location, I strain my eyes and peer into the darkness. Nothing. Still nothing, but I'm sure it was there.

Another motion to my right, and I jerk my attention in that direction, but the instant I do, the motion is on my left.

Something is playing with me. I growl, low in my throat as my tail goes still. Something would dare? I am the predator. I don't want to wake her, so I wait and watch. The shadows stir, my muscles tense, ready.

As something bursts from the darkness, I leap, and in a single motion sweep Amara behind me. She yelps in shock and surprise. I grab the blur heading for my throat, my fingers sinking into soft flesh.

SCREEEEE!

The creature screeches as my fingers close. It struggles in my grip, claws sliding across my protective scales. Behind it more things leap out of the shadows. Too many for me to grab them all.

"RAWR!" I roar in rage, pulling their attention to me.

I slam one thing with my tail, punch another with my free hand while throwing the one in my grip as far as I can. The battle is engaged. The screech and chitter. Claws scrabbling against the steel of the ship's construction.

Another one of the creatures leaps at my head. I duck and it passes overhead, hitting against the wall and causing a ringing sound.

"Look out!" Amara screams.

I duck again as I turn to her, scooping her up with one arm and backing up. We're too exposed. They can come at us from all sides. I haven't even figured out what it is that's attacking us, but whatever it is, they're clearly hungry and wanting to make a meal of us.

Holding her with one arm, I back into a corner then set her down. She moves behind me and makes herself as small of a target as she can. She's a brilliant female. I grab my lochaber off my back and whirl it in a defensive pattern, ready to take out the next attacker with lethal force.

The creatures continue to screech and their claws scrabble, echoing off the steel. One of them runs towards my left but retreats as soon as I turn to face it, but that leaves an opening for the one on my right.

That one leaps in, and razor-sharp teeth clamp down on the arm I bring up to block it. It locks down as I try to shake it free, but the teeth only dig in deeper. I lose my grip on my lochaber and it clatters to the floor.

I roar, rage and pain mixing, flinging my arm wildly, trying to get it to let go. I stumble to one side, thrown off by its weight. I slam it against the wall over and over. It grunts with each hit but doesn't let go.

Another monster jumps for my face, and I barely block it with my one free arm. It tries to get a bite on me too, but I'm able to move quick enough to avoid it. It falls to the floor on its side with a huff, then runs back into the shadows.

The creatures dart in and out while the one chews on my arm. The pain makes stars dance in my vision. I use feet and tail to keep the ones in the shadows at bay while continuing to slam the one chewing on my arm into whatever comes close enough for me to use. Crates fly around, the wall becomes dented, still it won't let go.

"SHIDAN!" Amara yells.

I whip around towards her. She has my lochaber, holding the point up and out. She stabs the air in front of her, and I see her plan. Whirling in a circle, I raise my arm, bringing the thing up with it, and then the blade slides through it.

The creature lets out a death scream then falls limp, but its teeth are stuck in my flesh. The added weight of my lochaber run through it and the loss of blood—I cannot keep my arm up. I let it drop limp to my side, focusing my attention on the remaining enemies.

They're less certain with the death now. They retreat into the shadows, but I stand ready for a fresh assault. The air is filled with a foul scent from the creatures' blood that will either drive them away or call more of them to the wounded one's aide.

Silence falls.

"Is it over?" Amara asks, gasping.

I don't answer, focusing to hear any hint of a sound. A final skittering sound, then nothing. I wait, listening to my breath coming in and out until I'm sure that they are gone.

"Yes," I say at last.

She exhales heavily. "Okay. Well, that was exciting."

I nod and retrieve my lochaber then explore the shadows, poking the sharp blade into them to make sure that they are truly gone. I do not want another surprise. I must protect her. My treasure.

"It is safe," I say, finally satisfied that the threat is over.

She grabs my face and pulls me around towards her. Her hands rest on my cheeks, her eyes gleam in the soft, silvery light. It accents her beauty.

"Shidan..." she trails off.

Silence falls across us like a warm blanket. It is almost comfortable except there is a wrongness between us. The wrongness is me. My memory, or lack of it. There's a word for the things that attacked us, I know it, but I have no idea what it is.

As a cold chill forms in my limbs, I jerk her closer, pulling her off her feet, and I kiss her. This is all I need. She is an anchor, the reason, she is all I need. The dragon rumbles in pleasure and my cock stiffens.

She returns the kiss, wrapping her arms around my neck. Our tongues dance together as my cock throbs with pent-up need. I grab her hair to pull her head back, breaking our kiss so I can lick my way down her neck.

Her breasts press hard against my chest. It's enticing, and though I know them well, they're still exotic. No Zmaj female has breasts exposed like hers. I want to taste them. She is mine.

She opens her shirt, leaning back in my arms, causing her breasts to thrust forward. I bury my face between the fleshy mounds. Her skin tastes of sweetness with a hint of spice. She moans as I lick every inch, squeezing her ass.

She moves her hips, grinding against my throbbing dick. The urge to bury myself in her is strong, but I hold off. My attention is for her breasts. I kiss up the left mound until the soft, brown tip is in my mouth. I tease it with my tongue, rolling it over and over, until it is as hard and stiff as my cock.

She groans as I flick it with my tongue, then I lick and kiss my way to the other side, repeating my action. I move back and forth between them until both are tight points. I carry her closer to the wall and pin her between myself and it, returning my lips to hers.

Our kiss is deep, passionate. A kiss to lose myself in.

She works her hips, her hands running through my hair, tugging and pulling. I push my hips against her, my hard cock crushed between us.

"Mine," I growl.

"Fuck me," she whispers in my ear. "Make me yours."

Primal instincts surge, and I don't hesitate. After dropping her to her feet, I spin her by her hips, so her ass is bowed out and pressing against me. I grab her pants with both hands and slide them down and off, dropping to my knees behind her as I do.

I trail my tongue up her leg as I straighten, tracing the swell of her ass. I shove my hand between her legs and force them to part as I trail my hand up the inside of her thigh to her womanhood.

Her wetness welcomes me. My fingers slide inside of her as I lick around her ass and down the crack. She rotates her hips as I drive fingers into her depths, and she moans.

I groan, my cock pounding, wanting release, but I won't give that to it yet.

My free hand finds her dangling tits, and I tease the tips while pushing my fingers in and out of her wet pussy. She gasps with pleasure, shuddering as sensation becomes the center of our universe.

Mine.

Primal claim. She is mine. No other may touch her.

I squeeze her tits, thrust my fingers in and out of her wetness until they are well coated, then I pull them out and slide them up the crack of her ass. I tease her rear entrance, covering it with the moistness.

She gasps but thrusts her ass back towards me, inviting.

Inviting my claim.

I slide my fingers back down and into her waiting pussy. She moans as I twirl them deep inside, teasing and filling, then slide them back out and up.

I work this over and over until her rear entrance is slick with her juices. My free hand drops my pants and my cock is stiff and ready. I place the head at her back door.

"Slow," she whispers.

My cock spasms, releasing its early juice to help ease its acceptance. The white cream coats her in preparation.

I push forward and she pushes back. The tip slides in and then stops. She moans and adjusts. She supports herself against the wall with both hands bending over further. The curve of her sides and the swell of her ass is beautiful. Perfect.

She shifts, one hand on the wall and reaches back to spread herself open further. Then she pushes back, slowly, until the first ridge of my cock slides into her rear. She yelps, stops, and I hold still, letting her adjust.

"Yes," she moans, her voice low and hoarse.

My secondary cocks is stiffening too. It's not designed for this, but then we've never done this. I'm so aroused I can't hold it down.

She pushes back again, and the second ridge of my prime

cock enters her. The tight warmth grips my dick. I close my eyes, throw my head back, and moan in pleasure.

"Mine," I growl.

"Take me," she hisses, pushing back again, but now my second cock is fully erect.

It pushes against her pussy, the tip sliding into her warm wetness. A groan escapes and I hiss.

Sex has never felt this good.

"Shidan!" she exclaims her pleasure and pushes back yet again.

My prime cock goes deeper into her rear, and my second pushes into her pussy. The two cocks rub against each other inside of her. The pleasure is so intense, stars explodes across my vision, and a shudder races down my spine.

Grabbing her hips, I hold position, letting us both adjust to the increased sensations. My prime cock spasms, leaking my seed but I'm far from ready to finish this.

I've never laid claim to her in this way. The sensation is extraordinary.

"Fuck," she gasps. "Fuck me."

I am hers as much as she is mine. I push in, claiming her, but her body is laying its claim on me also.

She is my treasure, I live for her. Her body takes my cocks deeper and deeper, until I'm fully seated inside her ass and her pussy.

She has her head down, panting as she leans against the wall. She moans yes, yes, yes over and over and I wait, letting her body accept the role we are asking of it.

I bring my tail around and tease her tits with it, massaging them as I shift my hips, adjusting my cocks inside of her.

"Do it," she orders. "Take me."

I pull back, still slow. I do not want to hurt her, and this is new. I only pull back part of the way then push back in. She moves with me, and they slide in easily.

I repeat the motion, concentrating, holding the pleasure aside from myself. The fog of the bijass crashes against me as the dragon roars excitement at staking its claim deeper than ever before.

"Yes," she gasps. "Oh god, that feels so good."

"Take me," I order, as I thrust in to seat fully in both her holes. "Mine."

I lightly slap her tits with my tail. My female. My treasure. My life.

Pulling back I hold the tips inside her holes, waiting. She bemoans the loss and pushes back against my cocks.

"Do it," she orders.

I thrust in hard, full depth, all the way to the ridge of my pelvis. Fully into her, and she yelps in surprise as she takes it.

"Yes!"

I thrust in, driving my cocks deep in both holes, making her mine. Becoming hers.

In, out, in out. The slapping of skin against skin as I thrust in is accented by my tail slapping her tits. She keeps one hand on the wall and with her now free hand she rubs her clit.

The fullness of her ass pleases my vision. I watch as my primary cock slides into her asshole. The sensation of my secondary cock in her pussy—its ridges on top rub against the underside of my primary cock. It makes her pussy and her asshole extra tight.

It's hard to hold back my orgasm. My cocks throb with need, but I won't let go. Not yet, no matter how much I want to fill her with my seed. Her womb is mine, and it's high time I filled it again.

"Yes, put that big dick in my ass," she moans, rubbing her clit faster. "Fill both my holes. Take me, Shidan. You're mine."

Hers. Always. I am hers.

I fuck her with wild abandon. Cocks driving in and out, tail teasing tits. One hand is slapping her ass, and with my other hand, I grab her hair and pull her head back.

I curl my tail up, caress across her throat, and she jerks her head forward to lick the tip of my tail.

As much as I'm fucking her, she's claiming me. My heart is hers and my body too. We belong one to another, and our bodies' coming together is a display of that love.

A shiver races through my limbs. I groan as she moans loudly.

"I'm there," she cries out. Then her body stiffens.

Her ass and pussy clamp down on my cocks. The orgasm overtakes me then. She cries out as her back arches, and she shudders. Both of my cocks pump their loads, filling her over-full, and pushing out more.

The dragon roars. I'm planting my seed. Marking her. Mine.

My wings open and close as the final shivers of orgasm race through my body, and then I'm spent.

"Wow," she gasps, coming out the other side of her own orgasm.

Slowly, I withdraw, then wrap my arms around her. I hold her tight, enclosing her in my arms, tail, and wings. She leans her head back and up, and we kiss. Our passion is physically spent, but our spiritual passion for each other knows no bounds.

I know she's mine, and I am hers.

Always.

9

AMARA

I'm sore when I wake up a few hours later but sore in that good, holy-hell-that-was-an-amazing-lay way. I can't stop the smile when I stand up and realize I'm a little bow-legged. Damn, he's never fucked me like that before. It was primal, instinctive, and so damn sexy.

We dress together, with plenty of touching and kissing. It's almost like everything is normal. Another day, work to be done, and all that. Except it's not.

Our mission here was a bust. There are no medications and we haven't found the machine that Addison wanted. It's clear to me that this place has been raided by more than us. The Zzlo, those alien assholes, have clearly taken anything they could salvage and sell too.

Most of the crates we've moved around are empty or have parts to machines that we don't have for them. It's a mess and the work here has been hard. Especially to come up empty handed. We're going to need another option.

Shidan is moving the final crates in our last, desperate attempt to uncover something that will help. I watch him work because at this point it's faster and easier to let him do the heavy lifting. All I would do is be in the way.

He grabs a crate, moves it over to me, and I unlatch it. When I open it there are pills. My heart leaps as my eyes widen.

"Is this it?" he asks.

"I don't know," I say. digging through them.

They have dozens of names, none of which mean anything to me. I don't know what else I expected. Maybe a magic bottle with a tag saying, "Drink me!" would be nice. Anything that makes it clear it will help.

"We'll take them to—" he cuts off, and I glance at him.

His mouth works, brow furrows, then he snaps his jaw shut. He shakes his head and smiles.

"Addison?" I ask, filling in for him.

"Of course," he says, still smiling, but the blankness in his eyes can't cover the truth.

"How bad is it?" I ask.

"I am fine," he says, moving to close the crate. "I should be able to rig straps to carry this back to—"

He does it again. This time I see something in his eyes, but my stomach drops, and bile rises in my throat.

"Shidan?"

He frowns, shaking his head. He lifts his hands then drops them to his side. His shoulders slump, and he won't look in my eyes.

"I…" he trails off.

"Yes?" I ask.

He looks up and meets my eyes.

"Where were we taking this?" he asks, pointing at the crate.

My heart leaps into my throat and tears fall. I can't stop them. I step around the crate and wrap my arms around his waist. I'm losing him. Faster and faster he's forgetting, and I don't know what to do. The fear is paralyzing but I can't just do nothing. There must be a cure.

"The City," I say, pushing words past the lump in my throat. He frowns and nods. "Come on, we need to move."

I help him shoulder the straps and get the crate up on his back. Climbing back out of the ship proves to be a challenge, but we overcome it together, and at last we're working our way across the desert.

"Hang on a minute," I say, stopping and wiping sweat from my brow with the sleeve of my blouse.

I take the waterskin off my side. The water is warm but wonderful, washing the grit from my mouth and throat. I hand the skin to Shidan. He takes it and stares.

"Drink," I encourage him. He stares at the skin, me, then the skin again. "Here."

I lift his hands so that the opening of the skin moves to his lips. He takes a drink himself then hands the skin back. I close my eyes, take a deep breath, and let it out slow. Stay calm. It's all going to work out.

All this started because of the Invaders. I shield my eyes and stare up into the reddish sky, trying to see past the glare of the suns. Somewhere, probably in orbit, is a ship. A ship full of alien invaders who want… something.

The something is the problem. They showed up after the meteor showers repeatedly rained glass-like material down on the planet. We thought they wanted the glass as they seemed to be gathering it, but the meteor showers have stopped, and they haven't gone away.

Ladon had a plan of some kind that he and Rosalind secretly cooked up. I know that much, and I've put together enough pieces to know that he went into the desert, and that's where he got sick. There was a new guy from the Order there at the time too.

So either Ladon's plan went wrong, and that made him sick,

or the Order aren't friendly like we've thought, and they infected him. If it's the latter, we're well and truly screwed. If it's the first, well, we're still screwed but maybe less?

Shidan moves next to me and places a hand on my lower back. I stop staring into space, turning to look at him. He's staring off across the empty desert seeing... what?

"What are you looking at?" I ask. He looks at me but doesn't answer. "Shidan?"

His jaw tenses, and he softly pushes me into motion, still silent. I walk at his urging. He moves his hand to my bicep, keeping me moving with him. He angles off to one side, the wrong direction for the City and keeps moving.

"Shidan, stop!" I say, jerking my arm free.

His face contorts as he turns to face me. His jaw is tense and fire burns in his eyes. He points at me, then moves his arm so its pointing in the direction he was taking us.

"No," I say. "Shidan, talk to me. What is happening?"

He frowns deeper, opens his mouth, then it snaps shut. His tail goes deathly still, and his wings fold in tight. There's a struggle happening in his eyes. He's at war with himself.

"Home," he says at last.

"Shidan," I say, moving closer to him and putting hands on his chest. "Home is this way."

I point indicating the direction to the City. He shakes his head and points back the other way.

"Home," he insists.

Pressure builds in my head, unshed tears, sinuses blocking up as I struggle to keep it together. None of that is going to get us through this. He needs me.

"Shidan," I touch his face, accenting my words. "Trust me. This way."

He frowns and a soft growl escapes his lips, but then his face softens as I run my fingers over it.

"A-ma-ra," he says, sounding my name out as if it's new to him.

"Amara," I say softly, one tear escaping. "Home. This way. Our son."

His eyes widen. "Son?" he shakes his head, frowning deeper and then his eyes clear. "Malcolm!"

He exclaims it, a declaration against the encroaching darkness that is claiming his mind.

"Yes!" I yell with him. "Our son. Malcolm. He needs us."

He rubs his head with both hands, mussing his hair, pulling at his horns then nods.

"Malcolm," he says, holding his hand out.

I take his hand and we run in the right direction. I focus on one foot in front of the other keeping my thoughts carefully under control. Despair flitters on the edges and one stray thought could bring it all crashing down.

The suns move across the sky, and we make progress towards home. As we climb a rise, I see movement to our left. Squinting I make out a pack of guster, one of the most dangerous predators on the planet. Shidan sees them too.

He drops my hand, grabs the lochaber off his back, and slides it out from under the crate he's carrying. He holds it in one hand then grabs my hand back, and we keep moving. With any luck, they're on the trail of some other prey.

I know he can fight them off, but it's dangerous for him and for me. I can't fight one of them. Each guster stands about five feet at the top of its elongated head. They walk on four legs with large webbed feet that let them move across the sand easily. They have hulking mounds on their backs with bony sharp spines protruding that ward off predators.

As if they have any predators. Maybe once they did, but now outside of the ginormous sand worms, we call zemlja and the Zmaj, they have none. Even the Zmaj avoid them if possible. They hunt in packs, making them more dangerous, and they will eat anything.

The pack disappears as we slide down the dune, and all I can do now is hope. The hair on the back of my neck stays on end for a long time, but we keep moving and nothing happens. I'll take my small miracles where I can get them.

No matter how long I've been here on Tajss the one thing I must never forget is how dangerous it is. It's human nature for 'normal' to become equivalent with safe. Our awareness lowers and we become complacent. Complacency is the same as a death wish here. Literally everything on this planet is willing, if not actively trying, to kill you.

One rule I learned early on. The prettier it is, the more deadly it probably is too. I'm relieved when we climb another dune and the glimmer on the horizon says the City is not far. The protective forcefield dome that covers it is a beacon, calling us home. Home to safety and, hopefully, a cure in the box Shidan carries.

"We're almost there," I say.

Shidan tilts his head looking at me as we walk. He doesn't respond and my stomach sinks. I'm helpless. Trapped in a battle against this invisible enemy that I can't do anything about. I hate being helpless.

"Shidan, damn it, stay with me," I curse. "You hear me? You fight this shit!"

He frowns, opens and shuts his mouth a few times, then nods.

"Amara," he says. "Malcolm."

The way he says our names makes me think of a chant, and it must be for him. As we keep walking, he mutters them over and over. Committing them to memory or holding on to them, I don't know, but I'm not going to interrupt him. Whatever it takes, my love. You stay with me.

At last we reach the City. The dome is cool to the touch as

we wait for the airlock door to open. Shidan stares at the panel, the door, the dome itself. When the door swishes open, he jumps, lochaber coming to a ready position.

"It's fine," I say, walking through the opening. "Come, come in."

He stares at the door for a long moment then back to me before he walks in. He doesn't put his lochaber away but does keep it at his side. The door cycles shut and the air around us wooshes. My ears pop as the pressure equalizes. Shidan growls, looking all around wide-eyed. I put a hand on his arm.

"It's okay," I say. "Stay calm."

The door on the opposite side opens, letting us into the City itself. A young guy is on duty today. I don't remember his name right off, but I do recognize him.

"He okay?" the guy asks.

"He'll be fine," I say.

"He sick?" the guy asks, eyes narrowing with suspicion.

"He's fine," I snap. "Now get back to work."

The guy's eyes widen as his cheeks flush. "Fine, damn, who died and made you Boss?"

Ignoring him, I take Shidan's hand and pull him through the city at something just short of a dead run. The empty streets allow for no distractions, and it doesn't take long before we're at the door to Addison's lab. I don't bother knocking before barging in, and instantly regret it.

"Wha—" Addison is cut off as everything happens at once.

We burst into the room. Melchior is standing with Addison, and it's obvious they were sharing a kiss when we enter. As soon as we step in, Shidan growls and the crate on his back drops to the floor.

BANG! It hits the floor as he leaps forward, lochaber at the ready.

Melchior reacts as fast as thought. He flings Addison aside

as he twists his body to avoid the blade of the lochaber. The lochaber slices through where he was a moment before.

"SHIDAN, NO!" I scream as Addison cries out too.

Loud banging accents the commotion in this room, echoing through the walls where Addison has locked away Ladon and Ormarr.

Shidan turns, following Melchior. The two Zmaj circle each other, and now Melchior has drawn his lochaber as well. They clash, the wooden shafts of their weapons clacking as they crash together with a speed too fast for my eyes to follow. The glinting of steel, the ringing crack of wood on wood and metal against metal. They're trying to kill each other.

"NO!" Addison and I scream in unison, but the two men ignore our cries.

They close again, seeking any opening. I have to stop him. He's out of control of himself, acting on primal instinct and the only way out of this is one of them is going to die. I can't have that. I do the only thing I can, no matter how incredibly stupid it probably is.

They part, circling each other, weapons held ready. I take a deep breath and act.

I leap between them at the same time they move to close again. The blade of Shidan's lochaber whishes up, barely missing my nose, as he jerks it away from his intended strike. I tense expecting a blade in my back from Melchior but he avoids stabbing me too.

"Stop!" I yell, putting my hands on Shidan's shoulders and pushing him back.

He takes a step, his eyes darting from me to Melchior. He growls, a deep rumble coming from his chest.

"What is happening!" Addison yells.

"Shidan no," I say, forcing my voice to exude a calm I don't have. "Friends. They're our friends. Do not attack. No."

Something shifts in his eyes, he frowns, his brow furrows and then he moves his mouth.

"Fr-ien-ds," he says, his mouth working to form the word.

"Friends," I repeat.

Understanding dawns on his face and with it I see fear. I throw myself around him and I can't hold back my tears. I squeeze him tight, sobbing. Slowly he wraps his arms around and holds me tight.

I let it go. The pent-up fear, frustration, all of it pouring out in giant sobs until I'm left empty and spent. He holds me, runs his hands through my hair, and remains silent. Silent because he has nothing to say or silent because he doesn't remember the words I don't know. That thought creates a new round of sobs but I've got no tears left.

Finally I straighten from his chest. I rub my face with both hands, wipe my sleeve over my eyes and dry my cheeks. Blinking several times to clear my vision I turn at last towards Melchior and Addison.

Addison is kneeling next to the crate and sorting through the contents. Melchior is staring off to one side obviously uncomfortable with the display but keeping himself positioned protectively between Addison and Shidan.

"Anything?" I ask, my throat raw.

Addison doesn't look up from her digging.

"Yes," she says and my heart leaps. "But nothing I think will help the guys." And my heart crashes along with my stomach. "There are medicines here that will be helpful, but not with why you went."

She shakes her head and rises to her feet.

"Nothing?" I ask.

She frowns and shakes her head then walks closer. I feel Shidan tense more than I see it so I turn around and put my hands on his chest. He looks into my eyes and relaxes, still silent.

"Can he speak?" Addison asks.

"Shidan?" I ask, passing the question to him.

"Yes," he says, but there's a hesitation and I can see him thinking before he speaks. He may be able to speak right now but he's losing it.

"Oh shit," I exclaim, whirling to face Addison. "Melchior! You're exposed."

"I know," Melchior says.

"I'm so sorry," I say. "We didn't know anyone else would be here."

Addison frowns and shakes her head. "It was a risk. We shouldn't have taken it. He was probably exposed by me anyway. He refused to stay away any longer."

"Mates?" Shidan growls, glaring at Melchior.

Melchior grimaces and nods.

"Good," Shidan says and at last he puts away his lochaber.

Melchior slides his own into place behind his back and the tension in the room drops for the first time since we burst in.

"What are we going to do now?" I ask Addison.

She yawns. Only now do I notice the heavy bags under her eyes, the sallowness of her skin, and the deep exhaustion clearly written on her face.

"I... I don't know," she sighs, shoulders slumping.

"When's the last time you slept?" I ask.

"I don't know that either," she admits. "Who has time?"

Addison throws her hands into the air and shakes her head. She looks about ready to cry too, which I understand. The two men stare at each other across the distance. Addison and I stand between them. She's as lost as I am but I'm a makeshift engineer. This is a problem and that means there must be a solution. I only have to figure it out.

"What about the Order?" I ask.

"I've reached out to them," Addison says. "They haven't had anything useful yet. They seem as lost as I am."

"Ask Khal," I say.

"I have," she says.

"Then ask again! If he hasn't given an answer demand one. We need to know what they know, if any damn thing."

"What I need," she says, rubbing her forehead. "Is a sample. I don't know Zmaj physiology enough to say what's not belonging in there and what does."

"How do I get you a sample?" I ask.

Addison chews her lip then begins pacing the room. I watch, waiting, seeing her work it through. There has to be an answer.

"We know it starts with Ladon," she says, talking out loud. "He's patient zero. He was exposed to something in the desert when he went out there. I don't know why he was out there. He was with that new Order member, the one who brought Ashlee to the City."

She stops pacing and stares at me. I hold my hands up defensively.

"I don't know anything you don't," I say.

It's not a total truth but we're not supposed to talk about it. I don't know I know all of it either anyway. Rosalind was vague about what he was doing out there so it's not like I have details to give if I felt I could. If that's where it started though, it gives me something I can do.

"I'm at my wits end," Addison sighs. "Ladon is completely regressed. He's primal. Ormarr is in bad shape as well and…"

She trails off staring at Shidan then shakes her head.

"Right," I say. "I'm talking to Rosalind. Let me see what I can find out about that first."

"Okay," Addison says. "I'll continue trying. See if I can come up with something."

"Good," I say, turning to look at Shidan.

"Are you okay?" I ask.

He stares blankly and that's all the answer I need. He's not okay, far from it. My chest tightens and my throat clenches.

"Am-ara," he says, sounding my name out.

He touches my cheek, his fingers cool against my skin. As I look in his eyes I see the one thing I've never thought I'd see from him. Fear.

"Can..." I can't force the words past the lump in my throat. Swallowing hard, I struggle to hold back my tears and try again. "Can we have a moment."

"Of course," Addison says.

She and Melchior leave the room. The sound of the door shutting behind them is the only mar on the absolute silence between us. I stare into his eyes. His beautiful, perfect eyes that have always shined with their absolute love for me. Even now, as he loses his memory, I see that fiery love.

Life is a series of moments. Some good, some hard, but this one I never saw coming. Nothing could have prepared me for this, I never thought I'd lose him.

"Shidan," I say. "Stay with me."

The tears I've been fighting with won't be held back any longer. He pulls me tight against his chest and I hug him tight. Holding on to him for dear life.

"Amara," he says, kissing the top of my head. "Treasure."

"Yes," I sob, swamped in a storm of emotions. "I can't lose you."

He grabs my shoulders and pushes me back so he's holding me far enough away our eyes meet. His jaw is tense, his eyes alight with passion and more.

"Never," he says. "Mine." It makes me cry harder. He hunches down so we're eye-to-eye. "Love. Eternal."

"Oh Shidan," I say, shaking my head I touch his face.

There is no forming words past the lump in my throat.

"The fog," he says, speaking with more clarity than he has in some time. "It's... eating the past. Harder to control... emotions. Nothing changes. You, me... our son."

He wipes the tears from my cheeks with his thumb. More fall to replace them. I swallow and nod.

"I love you," I say. "I can't do this without you."

"Always," he says. "This disease... we'll find cure, but it doesn't matter. I know you. My love for you cannot be taken."

I throw my arms around him again and jerk myself against his chest. We hold each other until I run out of tears and then a bit longer still. He doesn't let me go until at last I step back and we kiss. A simple kiss, an affirmation kiss. This isn't the kiss of rising passion but the kiss of soul mates. A kiss but more a symbol. Signifying love eternal. Sealing our place in each other's hearts for all of time.

I open the door to let Addison and Melchior in. No one says anything. The four of us stare at each other waiting for someone to make the first sound, say the first words.

"I'll go to Rosalind," I say at last unable to stand the heavy silence.

"Good," Addison says. "I'll keep working."

She glances at Shidan but doesn't say what's on her mind. She doesn't have to, we're thinking the same thing. I can't take him out. One he's a known carrier but two he's already attacked Melchior in a fit. What would he do out there? What if we ran into, well anyone?

"I will stay," Shidan says, seeing our dilemma and in his way handling it for me.

My heart swells with my love. Addison nods her agreement.

"We should have you stay..." she trails off looking at the other door in the room.

The one that the banging sounds have come from, the door that leads to the lock up where she's keeping the ones who are losing themselves to the virus. I open my mouth to object. I can't let him be locked up like that. It's too much like writing him off, giving up, but reality hits as fast as the thoughts occur.

It's the only answer. Shidan nods his agreement and we follow Addison through the door.

On the other side is a long white hallway. A single, dim, flickering light illuminates the hall causing long shadows to dance along the walls and floor. It's the perfect setting for most any horror vid. All I need now is a long moaning sound.

BANG! BANG!

I jump back, raising my hands defensively. Shidan throws his arms wide, wings spread, and tail straight up behind his back.

"It's Ladon," Addison says. "I'm sorry, he's trying to break out. It comes and goes."

"Can he?" I ask.

"No," Addison says.

The sounds stop and we walk down the hall. A door is on the left with a small window in it. Something slams against it jolting me again. Ladon's face presses against the window. He growls his face contorted with rage.

Bile rises in my throat. We have to help him. Addison moves quickly past as do Melchior and Shidan but I linger behind, staring. This is what I'm fighting. An almost silent killer that won't even leave him dead. It's worse, in ways, as if he's being turned into a zombie and there is nothing to be done.

I've never believed in impossible. I was the only female fighter pilot on a ship where they said a woman couldn't do the job. They said it was physically impossible and I proved them wrong. The impossible is what I do.

As the door closes on the love of my life the image of him staring out of that dirty glass window sears into my memory. My resolve redoubles. He was my savior before, now I will save him.

10

AMARA

"No," Rosalind says.

"What do you mean, no?" I yell.

"Amara," Rosalind sighs. "You know I can't allow what you're asking."

"I'm asking for a chance to save the damn day. It's time to be big damn heroes, and I don't see anyone else stepping up to the plate."

Rosalind's calm face is pissing me off. How can she sit here behind her big fancy desk and do nothing? I bound from my seat in front of it and pace the length of the office, hands balled into fists and punching the air to accentuate every word.

"I understand," Rosalind says. "But I can't put even more people at risk."

"We're losing them!" I scream, spinning to face her.

"Yes," Rosalind says.

My thoughts come to a stuttering stop. I snap my mouth shut, almost biting my tongue as it audibly clicks. She and I stare, one at the other, and I wait for her to say something more. Anything more. Some bright idea, a grand solution, something more than a concession that she's writing off the three Zmaj warriors who are sick and the others who might be, and we don't know it yet.

"That's it?" I ask when she says nothing more.

There's a twitch to her left eye. The lines on her face are deeper, the white hairs at her temple are more prominent. She blinks several times before she nods.

"Yes," she says. "We are doing all we can."

"No, we're not," I growl. "We can go to where Ladon got infected and get the stars-be-damned sample that Addison says will help her find a cure!"

"She doesn't know that," Rosalind says.

"She said it!"

"She said might," Rosalind points out.

"Which is better than nothing!"

"In this case, no, it's not," Rosalind says.

"My god, the crap they say about you is true, isn't it?" I say. I'm attacking blindly, not thinking about my words. "The Ice Queen coldly calculating without a single moment's consideration to the lives you're playing with. It's all the good of the many, and who cares if a few get ground up on the way?"

She flinches. It's not a lot, but I see the effect my words caused. I regret them.

"Is that all?" Rosalind asks.

"I'm sorry," I say. "I shouldn't have said that, I didn't mean it."

"It's fine," Rosalind says, pulling a stack of papers in front of herself and not looking at me.

"Rosalind," I say, voice trembling.

She looks up and her piercing, sharp gaze cuts through my anger and despair. I've hurt her, deeply, but she's not calling me on it. She doesn't say a word. Sitting, waiting, letting me say whatever it is I'm going to say. I've got one chance to fix this and no clue what to say. I'm not good with people, or words, or emotions, yet here I am. Swamped in the middle of all three.

I shake my head, press my lips together, and then do the only thing that I can still manage. I collapse back into the chair in front of her desk, head in my hands, and I cry. All of this is too much. I never, ever had a thought that I might lose Shidan. As much as I thought I didn't want him when he first chose me, now I can't imagine life without him.

All my frustration, my fear, and every other confused, messy emotion that doesn't make sense pours out in my tears. Rosalind's chair scrapes, and her boots click as she walks around the desk. She places a hand on my back and kneels next to me.

Silent, she pulls me into an embrace. She holds me as I melt down. All semblance of having it together gone. I'm lost. Lost without him and lost without a direction to go. Something, anything, useful to do. Some way or glimmer of hope that I can save him. Save him the way he's saved me so many times.

How many times can I cry? How many tears can I shed before I've got nothing left? Every time I think I'm done, and it's time to get into action, here comes another round of losing it. Emotions suck. Tears suck. Feeling helpless... I can't deal with this.

"What do I do?" I ask, as I manage to exhaust my tears yet again.

"We do," Rosalind corrects, tightening her grip on my shoulders. "You're not alone."

More tears swell, and it's all I can do to not start blubbering again. I'm a wreck.

"We," I say.

"I can't let anyone go back to where Ladon was most likely exposed," Rosalind says, cupping my cheek in her hand then returning to the chair behind her desk. "It's too dangerous. Even with the lockdown, we're looking at ten to fifteen percent of the population of the City is sick."

"That doesn't seem like that many," I say.

"It's not," Rosalind says. "Because I ordered the quarantine. If I hadn't, it could well be twenty, thirty, or even more. We can't afford to lose that many people. Our future hangs by a thread as it is. There are barely enough survivors, Zmaj and human, for there to be future generations. I can't put the future at risk for one or two people."

Her shoulders are hunched, head bowed, and she grips her own hands tightly as she speaks, but she doesn't shy away from the words. She's saying what she knows, what she believes. I believe her too. I've seen the numbers, the projections—all of us that serve on the Council have.

Genetically we need a minimum number of contributors to the gene pool to keep our two races from breeding ourselves out of existence. If we fall below it, we wouldn't even know while we're alive. Our great-great grandchildren would be the ones who suffer for our mistakes. The projects have them being the first generation to develop signs of genetic flaws that would open them up to untold diseases and deformities. It would only grow worse from there.

I know it, yet I don't care, not right now. Right now all I can think about is the idea of raising Malcolm on my own. What would I tell him? How do I explain to him that his dad went feral and we had to... what? Put him down? Banish him? Leave him to go live life in the desert on his own?

"What are we supposed to do?" I ask, voice cracking.

Rosalind sighs and shakes her head. "There are no easy answers. We need a cure, fast."

"And if we don't get Addison what she needs, we'll never have one!"

Rosalind arches an eyebrow watching me lose my temper, again. I've worked really hard to control my temper. So much for all that work, but if there's a time to lose your cool, then now is it.

"I understand," Rosalind says at last. "That doesn't change

the facts. I cannot expose someone else, not until we know more."

"Protective gear," I burst out.

"What gear?" Rosalind asks. "Do you think I haven't thought of that? If we had some kind of gear, I would have had someone out there after Ladon fell ill."

"I'll go," I say. "I'm already infected, if humans can get it, so I'll go. No one else will risk being exposed."

"That would be too stupid to live, Amara," Rosalind says shaking her head. "You can't go into the desert of Tajss alone, and I can't send a Zmaj with you. They might lose it while you're out there, and I'd lose both of you."

Rubbing the back of my neck, I come up with and discard a dozen ideas. There has to be an answer. Something.

"The Order," I say. "Addison says they haven't given her any definitive answers."

"Go on," Rosalind says.

"I'll go to them," I say. "I'll get the answers, if they know them."

Rosalind shakes her head. "And who would go to protect you?"

"I don't need protection, I need Shidan!"

I slam my fists onto her desk. Stupid. My hands throb with pain, and Rosalind isn't bothered in the least by my outburst.

"How bad is he?" Rosalind asks.

I drop back into the seat and lean back, rolling my shoulders and head to try and ease the tension headache.

"He's not terrible, yet," I say.

"That's not an answer," she says.

"He's losing speech," I say, meeting her gaze. "I don't know how long it will take. Addison didn't seem to know either. He fought with Melchior the moment he saw him. He's becoming... primal."

Rosalind nods. "That is the pattern."

"The pattern," I snort. "A pattern of three, but poor Amara happens to be part of the statistic."

"No one thinks of you as 'poor Amara,'" Rosalind says. "How many days since he showed signs?"

"Four? I think," I say.

Rosalind frowns. "You're right. We need to stop this, understand it, and handle it. I have no doubt a sample will help Addison immensely. There might be time."

"Time for what?" I ask.

Rosalind drums her fingers on the desk. She's considering something. I wait, letting her work it out for herself.

"To send him with you," she says.

"Seriously?" I ask.

"Of course," she says. "If the pattern holds, which admittedly our pattern pool is small, he'll grow worse, but he should have four, maybe five days before he completely regresses. That's enough time."

"Where do I go?" I ask, grabbing the opportunity before she can change her mind.

She opens a cabinet behind her, pulls out a rough piece of paper, and spreads it across the desk.

"Here," she says, pointing to a spot on the map.

"There's nothing there. What big surprise was Ladon looking for there? I thought he was getting something to help with the Invaders."

"He was," Rosalind says. "A bomb."

"There's a bomb here, in the middle of the empty desert?"

"Possibly," Rosalind says. "Apparently there used to be a military installation there. Ladon hoped to find a functional missile that we could fire at the Invaders' ship that is orbiting the planet."

"Uh, wow," I say, shaking my head.

That's more than I knew about it, and I'm a bit shocked. We can barely keep water running in the City, but they had a bright idea to fire a missile? I'm not sure how they thought that would ever work.

"Keep that a secret," Rosalind says. "It was a long shot, and I don't need more rumors burning the ears of the citizens."

"Yeah, I get it," I say. "What protective gear do we have?"

"Nothing," Rosalind says. "Maybe a mask or two, but I don't think anything we have is going to be effective. You'll be in a hotspot. You'll have to find where Ladon was trying to breach into the facility and collect samples of the sand, the air, and anything else that you find lying around."

"Done," I say.

"And Amara," she says.

"Yeah?"

"Be careful," she says, taking her hand off the map and letting it roll up.

She picks up the roll and holds it out to me. I take it, and our fingers touch. We stare at each other until she gives me a nod, and on instinct I come to attention and salute. She returns the salute. She is the Lady General, and part of me will always be a fighter pilot under her command.

11

SHIDAN

*T*he fog is thick in my head. Thought isn't easy, so I'm focusing on one thing at a time. Amara. Malcolm. Family. They are my mantra. I say her name and picture her. I say my son's name and picture him. Mentally, I'm clinging to those pictures.

The bijass is laying claim to the past. Urges hit me out of nowhere, and it's all I can do not to act on them. I stopped myself from grabbing her and running away many times already, stopping when I regain control. Amara tightens her grip on my hand. Focusing on her helps.

The dragon shifts, swirling in my core, rumbling with pleasure. She is my treasure. The one to be protected, valued, cared for—she is mine. It pleases my dragon to have such a strong and powerful mate. She is everything I would ever have dared to dream.

Amara stares at the paper in her hand, looks across the blowing sands then back to it. Her brow furrows, creasing the gap between her eyebrows. She shakes her head then rolls the paper up and slides it into the pack on her back.

"We should be close," she says.

I step towards her, reaching for her, then stop myself. No. I cannot steal her away. We are doing something... important.

"Close?" I ask.

Focus. Here. Be with her. She smiles. It's dazzling. Brighter than the suns. She is mine. Must protect her.

"Yes," she says, touching my cheek. Her fingers are soft. So soft, delicate, a light touch. A female's touch. "Are you okay?"

Her voice is a whisper. Her eyes search mine, and I push back against the fog, grabbing onto what is me.

"Yes," I nod. "Amara, I love you."

Tears well in her eyes, and she wipes them away quickly, then nods.

"I love you," she says. "So damn much."

A thought comes. It's too big. It's a concept, a feeling, emotions, more. It won't fit into words, and I don't know how to tell her. It makes my tongue feel thick. The fog of the bijass surges, trying to steal it but the idea is too big to be lost.

"I..." How do I say this? What words will make her understand? "I'm sorry."

She stops, standing so still it's frightening. Her lip trembles, and more tears form in the corner of her eyes.

"Sorry?" she whispers.

I put my hands on her waist and stare into her beautiful, glistening eyes. I study every line of her face. Every line telling a story, ones we've shared, and now I'm doing this to her. It's unreal, unacceptable, and for the first time in my life, I'm lost. I can't fight what I can't see. I'm fighting for control of my own mind, my thoughts, and I'm losing.

It's better out there. Away from other males. When I saw Melchior, the fog took over. I reacted, and while I was near him I could barely control it. The instinct to fight him, prove my dominance, all to protect her.

"Yes," I nod. "Sorry."

It's a small word, too small to convey the concept, but I have to trust in her. In our connection, in the ties that bind us, that she will understand.

"No," she shakes her head. "No. You don't be sorry. You fight. You fight! We're not done."

"When I lose it," I say. "I won't remember, but I'll never forget you. You are my treasure. Always. Forever."

"Forever," she echoes, a tear streaking down her cheek. "Isn't over yet, damn it."

She wipes the tear away with her sleeve. Neither of us move, frozen into a moment of time. My chest swells until it hurts. My love for her is too much for my body to hold in. It has to burst out, go somewhere.

The wind picks up, blowing sand into our faces and breaking the moment. Amara turns away to protect her eyes while I close the outer lid of mine to shield them. It's then I see a glint a few strides away.

"There," I say pointing.

I want to say more but the words I want to say are swept away by the thickening fog. Amara waits for the breeze to die down then turns and follows my pointing arm.

"Good!" she exclaims. "Let's put on our protective gear."

I don't understand what she means. She slides the pack off her back and opens it up. I watch, feeling like I should know what she's doing and what she's talking about, but there's nothing but a blank and a vague sense of loss.

She pulls out two masks and holds one out towards me. I know it's called a mask, but what to do with it is gone. I take it and turn it over in my hands, studying it. I know this. It's black, but there is this clear area here. I'm supposed to...

Amara slides the one in her hand over her head, and that makes it clear. I'm supposed to wear it! I slide it on to my head, mimicking her. It doesn't sit well. I can't get it fully onto my face, my horns are in the way. I tug at it, frustration growing, until I'm jerking it around.

"Here, let me help," Amara says.

She reaches up and does something I can't see. A few moments later and the mask is sitting on my face and I can see again. She takes my hand and together we walk towards our goal. As we approach, it's easy to see why we were having a hard time finding it. There are no landmarks. It's a hole in the sand, one that is partly filled back in, which makes it even more difficult.

We stand over it, our breaths loud through the weird mask we're wearing and stare. At the bottom of the hole that's been dug in the sand I can see metal. The metal is marred by deep gouges and scratches but there is nothing beyond that to indicate its purpose or use.

"Now?" I ask.

The bijass swells and recedes making it hard to think. I don't know what we should be doing. Do I attack it? Tear this thing down?

Amara drops down into the hole and puts her face close to it. She studies it this way for some time, then looks up and reaches a hand to me. I take it and pull her out of the hole.

"It's a seam," she says. "Ladon cracked it open, and that let out air, is my guess. The virus, the poison, whatever it is that's making you sick was in that air. He breathed it in, and then he carried it back to the City."

I nod, but her words don't make sense. There are a lot of them, but there is no picture in my head to go with them. They don't add up to… anything. A frown forms on my face as I try to make the words make sense. Every time I'm about to get it, the fog surges forward and washes away the thought.

I growl as frustration builds inside me heading towards anger, and with anger the fog covering my thoughts increases. Amara lays her hand on my cheek and that pulls my attention to her. The fog recedes and the anger lessens.

"What do?" I ask.

She shakes her head. "I don't know."

We stare at the glinting metal. An urge to tear at the metal surges, and I step forward, grabbing the lochaber off my back. I grip the shaft in both hands and raise it over my head in a fast motion, slamming the blade against the metal.

CLANG!

"Open," I growl, raising my weapon again and slamming it with even greater force.

The fog swells, eating thought, dispelling everything. I will win. I am the most powerful, I cannot be stopped. I hit it again then again and yet again.

"Shidan!" Amara screams.

I see her out of the corner of my vision. Her eyes are wide, mouth open, and she's moving back and away. Moisture streams down her cheeks, and her face is red. Moisture, word. There's a word for it.

It flits through my head, and I'm unable to latch on to it. The anger rages but that word... it cuts through the haze. She's crying. The word is crying.

A uniquely human thing to do. Zmaj do not cry. We are not capable of it. When I first saw a human cry, I thought it was wasteful, dangerous even. Tajss is a desert. Wasting water is the gravest of sins.

Amara's tears, though, they express depths of emotion that touch my soul. I've found myself, at times, being envious of her ability to shed tears.

They cut through my rage. I'm left empty and once more envious. The pressure in my head, the tightness in my chest, maybe they would ease if I could cry. It's a moot point, but looking at her, knowing I caused her pain and fear, it creates so much tension I want to explode.

I drop my lochaber and leap out of the hole, drifting down to land next to her. I pull her into my arms and hold her. I can't form words, all I can do is hold her, squeeze her, never let her go. This illness is bad for me, but it's worse for her.

I won't know when I lose it. It's happening, and I barely notice it until I see the effect on her. The fear, the loss, the anger, when I see it in her, then I know something is wrong. It's a silent killer that makes me feel impotent. That causes my dragon to stir, and with it, the fog of the bijass grows thicker.

I don't know how to fight what's happening in my head, so I do the only thing I can. I hold her, for all my life, but more for hers and for Malcolm's. She squeezes me every bit as tight as I do her. We hold each other for I don't know how long, but at long last, she straightens then pulls back.

Amara stares past me, into the hole beside us, frowning. Fog covers my thoughts once more, and now it seems thicker than ever. It's insidious, slipping in and around, covering over rational thought.

"We have to get in there," Amara says. "I don't have a way to capture air, but there's something in there that started this. We have to find it, take it back to Addison. You made progress—look! That crack is wider. Maybe we can pry it open?"

I see what she's talking about and nod. I land in the hole next to the broken seam. It's barely enough for me to slide my fingers in and get a tenuous grip. I do and pull, roaring as I put my body to work.

Metal creaks, groans, and moves the slightest bit. My fingers slip, and I fall backwards, landing on my tail. The pain shoots up my spine, and the red rage grabs at my consciousness. I growl but push back.

"Are you okay?" Amara asks.

I don't answer. Words are too hard. Instead I slide my fingers back into the crack and get a little better grip this time. Lifting with my legs, I pull again. My muscles scream as I strain, but then the metal screeches and it opens a little more.

A stale, musty scent wafts out of the opening along with

clouds of dust. It makes my throat itch, and then I'm coughing. I have to stop and wait to catch my breath when it passes. Amara is speaking. I hear her, but I don't understand.

I look up at her, and her mouth is moving. Is she speaking another language? It doesn't matter. She needs to get in here. I will do this.

I take up my position again, setting my feet, the claws of my toes clacking against the metal. I take a deep breath and exhale it violently as I pull. I groan, strain, and pull harder and harder. Dig deep, more, strain, and then the screech fills my ears, and the metal plate tears away in my hands.

I lift it over my head and throw it in triumph. It flies out of the hole and across the desert. I roar in victory, holding my hands above my head, fists closed, wings spread. The female stares with wide eyes as if something is wrong.

Her mouth moves. Sounds come out. My female. My treasure. Forever. Mine. Must take her.

She slides down the sand into the hole and moves to stand next to the opening with me. She places a hand on my back. Her touch radiates warmth. I grumble my pleasure, turning toward her. She points into the opening and emits more sounds.

She wants to go down, into the hole.

My female wants. I will give her what she wants. She is mine and pleasing her is my duty. I sweep her into my arms, fold my wings around us and drop into the hole. She screams, clinging to my neck.

12

AMARA

*H*e grabs me so quickly I yelp, but then we're dropping into the hole. My stomach is left up top, and I scream in surprise.

As we drop into the darkness, he opens his wings, and our flat-out drop becomes a drifting glide down towards whatever is waiting for us at the bottom. I tighten my grip on his neck, holding like glue and putting my trust into him.

The hole above is the only source of light, and it pools on the floor way below us. We're drifting down in a circling motion. My eyes adjust as we drop lower, growing used to the dimness. As far as I can tell, it's an open area, but there are shadowy outlines of objects dotting the floor.

My stomach finally catches up with us about the time we land. Shidan doesn't put me down, turning in a circle and growling while keeping me in his arms.

"Danger?" I ask.

He doesn't answer or stop what he's doing. I wriggle in his grip because if there is something dangerous down here, I want him to have his hands free to deal with it. He growls louder, looks down, then finally sets me on my feet.

He doesn't answer though. No words. When I look into his eyes, the bright light is dim. He's regressing further and faster. Swallowing hard, I do the only thing I can. I get into action. I put my hands on his shoulders and turn him around so I can access the pack he has. I pull out a torch, then hold it up in front of him.

"Light?" I ask.

He stares and frowns. I mimic blowing fire out of my mouth and that seems to get through to him. He burps a ball of fire that lights the torch.

"Okay," I say, with a heavy exhale. "Let's do this."

I take his hand in mine for reassurance as much as anything, and, choosing a random direction, go left.

We're in a large room. It might have been a hangar space at some point. Rosalind said that this was supposed to be a naval station before the Devastation. Ladon was hoping to find a workable missile, so a hangar makes sense.

There are no ships though, or at least none of a design I recognize. The space is filled with massive containers. Each one is an oblong cylinder that is around ten feet long and approximately five feet wide. There are rows and rows and rows of them. Dozens if not hundreds. It's impossible to tell because I can't see how far they go in all directions.

Squeezing Shidan's hand, I move to closer to one of the containers. It's so tall I can't see the top of it. The metal is covered in thick dust. I wipe some of the filth away to reveal a plate.

XO-10560-SAM

"What does that mean?" I mutter. "Lift me up?"

I ask Shidan, but he doesn't seem to get it. I mime what I want from him, and he grabs me by my waist and all but throws me into the air. The cylinder curves around, but on top there is what appears to be a broken glass window.

"Closer," I ask, using hand gestures to get him to understand.

When he has me close enough, I step on top of the container and kneel down. I shift the torch to my other hand and move it closer to the opening. As the light illuminates the inside of the container, I scream and fall backwards.

Shidan catches me and growls, moving me behind him in what feels like a single motion. He's ready for a fight instantly.

"No," I say, shaking my head. "It's fine. I was scared, that's all."

I rest a hand on his back trying to get my breath back. My heart is pitter-pattering as I try to stop the shaking that comes with too much adrenaline too fast. Shidan looks over his shoulder then turns around.

"Scared," I say again. "It's nothing. It's okay."

I don't know what I saw in there. It looked like a desiccated husk of... something. It shouldn't have scared me so much, but I didn't expect those glassy, empty eyes to be looking back at me. I push my hair out of my face and steel my resolve.

"Up," I say.

Shidan's eyes narrow and he frowns. The moment he does, my heart shatters and I can't catch my breath.

"Shidan?" I ask, touching his face. "My love?"

Something flickers in his eyes, a hint of the old him. The him of not so long ago, the man I love more than life itself. His mouth works, and on an impulse, I lift up on the balls of my feet and kiss him.

"A-ma-ra," he says, sounding my name out as if it's hard to say.

"Yes, my love," I say. "Fight it, you hear me? Fight it. You stay with me."

"Stay. Love. Treasure," he says.

"That's right," I assure him. "Your treasure. Stay here, with me. Now lift me up there again. WE have to find something for Addison to cure you."

He takes me by my waist and lifts me back onto the cylinder. This time I'm not going to be taken by surprise. I plant the torch where it hangs over the broken window so I can see, then get a sample kit out of my pack.

This is disgusting, but for Shidan I'll do anything. Including taking samples of desiccated, dead flesh. I scrape the samples into the tube and seal it, then carefully replace it. I don't know if this is what we're looking for or not, and there's still a lot of space to explore.

"I'm coming down," I say, grabbing the torch.

When I scoot to the side of the cylinder, Shidan has his arms outstretched waiting for me. I slide down into his arms, and he squeezes me tight before he puts me down. The next cylinder is still sealed, but through the dirty window I see what looks like a Zmaj.

We go from cylinder to cylinder with Shidan lifting me up onto each one, making our way slowly to the wall. Something keeps bugging me. It's tugging at my awareness, something I should notice or have noticed but haven't put together yet. It hits me, and I stumble to a stop.

"Do you hear that?" I ask.

"A-ma-ra," Shidan answers. "No."

I close my eyes and listen. There, it's soft, so soft I didn't notice it. A background noise, a low hum. Turning in a circle, I try to locate a source, but it's everywhere. I step over to the next cylinder and rest my hands on it, closing my eyes again.

"These things are on!" I exclaim.

"On...?" Shidan drags out the single syllable then makes it a question.

"On! They're running! What in the hell is this place?"

Looking in the windows of these tubes isn't giving the

answers I need, so it's time to take a different tack. I grab Shidan's hand and run down the row. When we reach the wall, the torch shows that there's a painted line running down the middle point of it stretching off in both directions.

I choose left, because all true adventurers always go left, or so I heard somewhere at some point. Mostly I don't have a better direction to go as they both look the same. Dark and creepy. I keep pulling Shidan along with me as I run. I'm onto something and I know it. I don't know what, but this is big. Super big. Now to figure out what 'this' is.

The further we go, the more the hugeness of the area hits me. If this was a military base, then this was a giant space. It's impossible to grasp the size fully with the small pool of light cast by my torch. A large, Zmaj-sized door appears in the wall. A sign on it reads, *Laboratory*.

Shidan touches the sign, running his fingers over it but he doesn't say anything. Emotions hit me like a jet fighter, punching straight into my guts. My throat closes and tears fall before I know what's happening. Seeing him like this makes me panic, I want to shut down, curl into a ball and pray for it to go away. It's a stupid urge, and I'm not going to give in. I can't. He needs me, and I'm going to handle this for him.

"Come on," I choke out, pulling him through the door.

Instinctively, I feel along the wall for a switch. Those things out there are powered. Does that mean there is power for the entire place?

I touch something metallic and cool. I fumble with it a moment, and then there's a soft click. Nothing happens. Damn it. I sigh heavily, then the room lights up, and stars dance in my vision.

"Argh!" Shidan growls, shielding his eyes and grabbing me with one arm, pulling me close.

"It's okay," I yell.

He's squeezing me too tight, it hurts, but he's holding me tight with one arm, his other closed fist held up defensively. He backs up to the wall and holds me there until at last he grunts and eases his grip. I slide to my feet rubbing my bruised ribs.

His tail twitches incessantly from side to side and his wings rustle. He's on high alert, nervous is what I would normally call it when he's like this. There's a feeling, though, that is different than what I'm used to with him. Something more primal that exudes from his posture and stance.

I struggle to keep tears at bay. This isn't the time or the place. Forcing my attention off of my love, I look at the room we're in for the first time. My stomach clenches tight, and my head pounds.

"Holy shit," I say, bile rising in my throat.

This is a horror show. A mad scientist lab. I can't comprehend what I'm looking at. Shiny steel tables are covered with equipment not dissimilar to what I would have seen on the ship in the med bays. There are five double rows of the long tables marching in even order down the middle of the room. An aisle between the rows leads to the back where there is an operating table. A big one, a Zmaj-sized one.

Along the walls of the room are upright tubes filled with bubbling green liquid. Each of them has a light inside that illuminates their contents which are the horrifying part. There are... people in there. Well, alien people, but people, floating in the liquid with tubes coming out of them.

Almost against my own will, not wanting to see but having to, I move to the closest one. A Zmaj floats inside but he's not normal. Instead he has two extra sets of arms that look like they belong to one of the Invaders. The surgery scars are clear on his sides where the arms are attached.

I swallow hard to force bile down. Shidan doesn't speak or react in any way that I can pick up on. He stares at the tube then touches the glass. When I move to look at him more directly, I see the next tube over and I can't hold back the sick that rises. Turning quickly I get rid of the stomach acid.

Shidan grabs my hair and holds it back. Like he did when I was pregnant with Malcolm. I can't hold back the tears. Turning to him, I throw my arms around his chest and squeeze, hiding my face in his abs.

"What are they doing here?" I ask, knowing he most likely will not answer me.

The other tube holds an Invader, and four of its arms have been removed. It's clear to see they took them off of it and grafted them to the Zmaj. I've seen all I want to, but I need to find more samples or anything that will help Shidan and the others.

Pulling myself together I stand up and do my best to ignore the tubes along the walls. I can't imagine the horror, the pain that these people were put through. It makes my skin crawl. The Zmaj that we know are all honorable, above reproach, how can I reconcile the men I know with ones who would do this?

How different was this world before the Devastation?

There's nothing I can do about that or with that information right now. I have to focus on finding answers to the problems at hand, not the ones being raised. Grabbing Shidan by his shoulders I turn him to face me.

"Papers," I say. "Find papers."

He frowns, brow furrowing, then nods. I push him away and he moves towards the tables. I set off in the opposite direction doing my own search. I don't know if there will be papers but it's something simple I can have him help me look for.

While he searches the tables I spy cabinets on the opposite wall and make my way to them. I do my best to avoid looking in the tubes between me and them but it's not possible. The images sear into my mind.

When I have time I'll be back. I promise all your poor lost souls. Right now I have to save my man. I hope you understand.

Silently I make my vow. The cabinets won't open. I tug but they're locked so I jerk. They rattle loudly, but I'm not getting in that easy. I put my foot against one and pull on the handle with all I've got. My hand slips and I slam onto my back.

"OW!" I yell as my head cracks on the floor.

Shidan is looming over me in an instant, growling. He helps me to my feet then glares at the cabinet. He grabs the handle.

"It's locked," I say at the same time his muscles bulge and he grumbles.

The door flies off its hinges, and he throws it across the room.

"Show off," I mutter under my breath, but I smile, grateful for his strength. The inside of the cabinet is filled with pills and vials of liquids, hundreds of them. "Jackpot!"

Shidan smiles and nods. "Good?"

"Yes!" I exclaim.

There has to be something among these that will be a cure. Out of all this horror that surrounds us, there must be some glimmer of hope, and this is it. I'm sure of it. I set about packing everything in the cabinet into our bags. Shidan may be regressing, but he's still smart. He sees what I'm doing and helps.

Once we're done with one cabinet I have him open the others and I take everything we can fit into our packs. We run out of room before we get everything there is, but I've prioritized what looks like medicine and then journals that will hopefully be understandable to Addison. When I look through them, they don't make a bit of sense, but I've got no medical training at all.

The bags are fully loaded, and that's all we're going to be able to take. Shidan lifts the biggest of them and settles it onto his back between his wings. He rolls his shoulders and shifts around until he's satisfied, then he tests pulling his lochaber out from under it and adjusts more.

"Ready?" I ask when he stops adjusting.

He looks at me, and I can see the gears turning behind his eyes. "Yes."

I smile and touch his face. My heart swells with pride and love, but the only thing that's going to save him is hopefully in one of these bags. I let him lead the way back to where we came in. Standing under the opening that he ripped through and looking up, my heart sinks. There is no way we're going to get up there. It's way far out of reach.

"Crap," I say.

There are underground tunnels in the City. I spent a lot of time in them when I was working to get the electricity running, but I never found them to go this far out. If they do, then the entrance is well hidden.

I don't think that's likely. If you're doing god-awful experiments on your own kind, then I doubt you'll have easy access for anyone and everyone. At least I hope they were secret experiments. I can't imagine the Zmaj men I know being okay with this kind of... well, torture is the only word that fits.

Why I didn't think of this before dropping into this black pit, I don't know. A moment of pure stupidity. Ugh. Okay, there has to be a way out. They didn't tear open their roof to move things in and out, that's only logical.

"We have to find a way out," I say.

"Out," Shidan repeats, so I nod.

"Out," I repeat and point at the hole above. He looks up and shakes his head.

"Far."

"Exactly," I say.

This room is still dark, the lights were for the other room only. So I get out my torch and have Shidan light it again. One way or another, we're not done yet. We'll find a way out if for no other reason than we have to.

Shidan grunts, growls, and then heads off, not needing the torchlight. I follow him doing my best to hold to the last glimmers of hope that I'll be back to Addison in time for him to benefit from the cure. The cure that is still only a hope itself.

13

SHIDAN

*T*he fog is thicker. Harder to think clearly. I understand Amara, I think, but when I try to answer her the words won't come. Disconnected images flash through my thoughts.

Amara and me, kissing.

Her yelling, angry at me, I've done... something.

Our... son? Playing. Running.

Protect. Must protect.

Along with every beating of my hearts, every breath is the drumming need. The singular urge of what I must do. I struggle with it, resisting the demand that I take her away to safety. This space we're in is too big. There are too many places for enemies to hide. The constant sense of danger is stretching my nerves, making my scales itch.

I scratch at the back of my neck as I try to keep looking in every direction at once. The tension in my shoulders creates a headache, but I ignore the discomfort. That, at least, is easy to do. I have so much else to put my attention on.

The flickering light of her torch affects my dark vision, but I know she needs it. I do too, I think. I can't see in total darkness, but the flickering is causing shadows to dance. I keep seeing things at the corner of my vision, and then stop to make sure it is not a threat.

It's so quiet, every step we take is like a violation of some unknown sanctity. Under the deep fog that not only covers my memories of long ago, but now is eating the current, something pulses. As if, almost, I know this place?

Have I been here before? It seems like something I would remember if I had.

"What's that up there?" Amara asks.

I see the direction she is pointing and stop, staring until my eyes can adjust. It might be a light, dim but the most hope we've had of getting out of here. I adjust our path, making our way around more machines, more things that tug at the strings of memory.

As we get closer it solidifies into a bit of light seeping underneath a door. This door is cool to the touch, cooler than it should be. I look at Amara and need to make her understand. Words, there are words I need for this.

"St-ay," I find it.

I motion with my hands in a patting gesture hoping it makes sense to her. I want to look in this door first. She nods understanding so I draw my lochaber off my back and then push the door open.

A bright light streams through the opening so I stop and wait for my eyes to grow accustomed. Only then do I step through and let the door close behind me.

The room I'm in is smaller with machines along the wall. There is a whirring sound and a thrum that I can feel more than hear. Since there is no threat apparent, I push the door open and motion for Amara to join me in the room.

"Control room?" she asks.

I hear the words and they make sense in a way, but then they don't. Control. I know control, but what does control have to do with a room? Something beeps loudly, jerking my attention off the problem of understanding her words. A light flashes on one of the machines.

Amara walks over and then pulls out a stool and sits in front of the thing. She touches dials, switches, and buttons as if she knows what she is doing. I put my lochaber away, cross my arms over my chest, and wait.

A few moments grows longer and then longer still, before she sighs and runs her hands through her hair, shaking her head.

"I don't know," she says.

I move closer and rub her shoulders, working the tension out of them. She is mine. My treasure. An image of a nice, safe cave breaks free of the fog. There. I need to get her there. I move to grab her up and go, but stop myself.

No. We're on a mission. A higher purpose, there is a... need. I don't know what that need is, but it is real. We have to go back to the City. The City! Right, I remember the City. There is a sickness, the items on my back, they need them. I'm saving more than Amara.

Malcolm is there. That's why our son isn't with us. I have to get back to Malcolm. Suspicion stirs along with images of my son's smiling face. Did they steal him? No. Amara would never allow it. She would not be so calm, but the thought lingers.

"Are you okay?" Amara asks, startling me out of my dark thoughts.

She rises from the seat and turns to me, wrapping her arms tight around me. I embrace her, pulling her as close as our bodies will allow, burying the niggling concern. It can't be. Amara is my treasure, she would never put our son in danger.

"We should go," she says. "This place is going to need a lot more exploration than we have time for. I hoped that I'd figure a way out from these machines, but I've got nothing."

She glares at the machines, then takes my hand and pulls

me out of the room. I step ahead and lead the way, continuing the path we'd already started. I lead us through dark passages with the only light her torch. The longer we go, the more it feels like someone or something is watching us.

We find more rooms but not a way out or anything that holds my attention. Malcolm. My son holds my attention. Why would I ever leave my son behind? There must have been a reason, but I don't know it.

The dragon rumbles, pushing me to move faster. I can't shake the idea my son is in danger. Whispers batter through my thoughts, making me edgy. Amara talks off and on, but I don't have the attention to spare trying to understand her words.

We come to various intersections and have to decide which direction to continue. There is no clear answer, but to make sure we don't double back on ourselves, I use my lochaber to mark the path we chose on the wall before we move past.

My stomach churns with hunger, but I'm ignoring it until Amara pulls on my arm. "Shidan."

I stop moving and she smiles shaking her head. She touches my face with cool fingers. The storm in my thoughts calms. The dragon recedes, relaxing in the glory of my treasure. I lean into her touch and listen.

"I'm hungry," she says, staring deep into my eyes.

When I meet her gaze, I could lose myself in the beautiful pools of her eyes. I nod and slide the packs off my back. I dig in and find our supplies. We don't have much left, and so far there is nothing down here I can hunt to provide for her. Holding the small amount of food in my hand I look at it, and the dragon growls. The sound slips out before I can stop it, and Amara looks at me sidelong.

"Are you okay?" Amara asks.

It takes me a moment to figure out the words to say. "I am."

I give her several morsels of food and pretend to put some

in my own mouth before I fold up the few remaining pieces and put them back into the bags. I don't want her to know how low our supplies have gotten. I can't let on to her that I'm worried.

As she eats, we resume walking. I extend my senses for any hint of a way out. After we've walked a long way and gone around many corners, I catch a waft of a scent on the air. It smells like fresh air, and the first glimmer of hope I've had in quite a while forms. I sniff the air and inhale deeply. Finally certain of a direction, I trace down the slight scent.

Moving faster and faster, I lead us along. As the scent grows stronger, I take her hand and quicken our pace. My hearts thrum with excitement, and soon she's running to keep up with my longer strides.

"Is that light?" she asks.

I'm too excited to figure out the words to say, so I squeeze her hand and continue pulling her along. We're in a hallway, and there are many doors, but I ignore them, chasing down the scent. The thin line of light at the end of the hall grows brighter as we get closer, then we're standing before a heavy set of doors.

There are symbols painted on the door, but they don't make sense to me, and I'm not going to take time to understand them right now. I push on the doors and they don't budge. After taking a step back, I throw myself against them and they reverberate, echoing with a hollow sound on the opposite side.

Red swells through my thoughts, and the dragon roars. I growl, backing away from the doors. My hearts race. My muscles tense. I will not be stopped. I will dominate this.

"Wait," she says, but the anger overwhelms her voice.

I charge the doors, slamming into them with my shoulder. They shudder and dent at the force of impact, but do not open. I pound them with my fists, roaring in anger.

"SHIDAN!" Amara yells.

It slices through the haze of rage. A thin line of reason. Panting I turn to face her, struggling to control myself. She walks closer, oblivious to the danger of the dragon. Her fingers touch my face, warm, trailing down and across my chest. Silent she rises onto her toes and her lips press to mine.

The dragon resists, holding to its dominance, then as fast as that, the switch is thrown. Desire burns like an inferno inside. My prime cock is rock hard, and all my thoughts are for making love to her. No, not love, fucking. I want to fuck her. Thrust into her, rut, lay my claim on her. Mark her as mine.

My treasure. Mine.

I growl into our kiss, wrapping my arms around her and jerking her off her feet. She embraces me, her pussy pressing hard against my pulsing cock. Holding her with one arm, I use my free one to rip her shirt open, exposing her stunning tits. I bury my face between them, lavishing my attention on each of them in turn.

She moans, throwing her head back and pushing her chest forward. Her hands twine in my hair and she moves my head from one breast to the other. I give control to her, making sure of her pleasure by letting her guide my head.

I can't hold back my needs though. Together we go to war with our remaining clothes as our passions consume us. We fight our way free of them until at last I'm sliding into her. I sigh with relief as her body welcomes me in.

Crushing her against the wall, I pound her pussy. Thrusting in hard and fast. This isn't gentle lovemaking, this is dominance. Claiming. Primal.

She is mine. Mine by trial and mine by right. She gives herself to me, as I am the victor. As I slam my cock into her over and over, each thrust is a testament of my worthiness. The ultimate predator. The winner.

It isn't long at all before we're both crying out our pleasures, and then my seed is being spent into her, laying that most important claim. The claim on a future. A future we are projecting ourselves into by our primal actions.

Spent at last, we're left panting, clinging to each other, huffing in the aftermath of our joining. She kisses my neck and runs her fingers through my hair. The primal haze recedes some, letting logic and thought assert itself once more.

We're trapped in this maze, and I have no way to provide for her. There will be no future if I don't get us out of here.

That sobering thought drives me. I put her back on her feet and we dress. She's smiling, touching my face and chest. She says words, but they don't mean anything to me. I know she is satisfied and that is good, but now what matters is freedom. Red skies over our heads, and the warmth of the double suns beating against my scales.

Room to run, to hunt, to protect her. Our son. He should be with us. It's an empty ache that demands to be filled.

Dressed, I turn my somewhat more rational attention to the doors. They're marred by deep dents, but they've held against my rage. A sinking feeling settles over my stomach as I stare at the barrier blocking our way forward.

"We need leverage," Amara says.

I try to understand, but words and symbols aren't forming together in my thoughts. Rage thrums underneath every thought, barely contained. It's a constant struggle to not give in to its demands. She walks back down the hallway and then peeks into one of the doors.

I rush to her side. We haven't explored these side rooms. I do not know if there is danger hiding in there. I pull her back away from the opening.

"Hey!" she cries out.

I hold up my hand and shake my head. She frowns, eyes narrowing, anger making the vein on the side of her head pulse. I ignore her and enter the room first, taking a careful look through the dim rooms to make sure that there is no threat to her.

"You didn't have to do that," she says entering the room behind me.

Fortunately, there is no threat in the room. There are many tables, chairs, and machines. So many machines. Amara digs through the room while I stand watch for any threats.

"Found it!" she exclaims, holding up a long tube of metal. "I think this will fix it."

She rushes past me and out of the room. I follow in her wake. She goes to the damaged doors and inserts one end of the metal tube into the small crack between them. She strains, grunting, but it doesn't make a difference.

"Are you going to watch or help?" she snaps.

I take a hold on the bar as well and then pull along with her. A loud screech echoes down the hall as the doors slide open. The bar lets go and we both stumble back coming up against the wall before falling.

Amara laughs. Her laugh is beautiful. A tinkling sound that is a delight to hear. Her entire face lights up as she pushes off the wall and dusts her hands. Pride fills her face as she looks at the door.

"Got it," she says, and laughs.

I squeeze through the opening first. By turning sideways and holding my wings tightly closed, I manage to slide through, and Amara follows.

This is another large chamber, but different than the one we first entered. It's not as big and mostly seems to be empty. The light that we saw coming under the door is from overhead lights that are burning bright and illuminating the entire space.

I look at Amara and shake my head. The dragon rumbles and the urge to explode pushes in. I'm holding on, barely, when she touches my chest and murmurs soft sounds. We stand in silence for a moment, then something screeches behind us.

14

AMARA

I can feel the anger rolling off of him and see the struggle on his face as he tries to contain it. A sense of helplessness leaves me lost and reeling. I can't help him, which is overwhelming. I put my hands on his chest.

"Stay with me, please Shidan," I say. "I need you."

Something screeches, so loud it makes my ears ring. My skin crawls as he whirls around to face the new threat. I look past him, and there's nothing coming from that direction. The large, empty chamber looks no different, and we can see clear to the walls.

There are sets of railings running around the middle, and I wonder what they are marking off. Shidan's tail is straight up and his wings are open while his hands clench into tight fists. I move to step past him, and he throws his arm out, blocking my way.

"Shidan, we need to look," I say, but he only growls. My anger flashes and I snap. "No. I'm not going to stand here like a little bitch and wait. We're going to look."

I shove past his arm and he grumbles but falls in with me.

Good. I don't want to go on my own, because I'm not stupid but I'm not going to be reactive. There has to be a way out of here. The screech sounds once more. This time I recognize that is has a metallic sound, like metal scraping against metal.

As we get closer to the yellow railing, I can see it surrounds a pit in the floor. I approach with caution, alert to any signs of danger, at least as much as I can be. The rail is meant to be protective because we're looking down into a black pit that goes deep into the earth. Really deep.

"Wow," I say.

The hole is huge. Probably thirty or forty feet around. Down in the hole there is something metal that comes to a point. I know what I'm looking at because I was a fighter pilot, though I never saw one this big. A missile. A really, really big missile. My mouth is dry, and a pressure headache is forming between my eyes. Rubbing my forehead, I take a step back and look up at the ceiling.

I stare until my eyes adjust to the overhead light and I can see it. A tell-tale seam in the ceiling. It can split open. The missile can be fired out.

The screech sounds and I jump, chills racing up and down my spine. Shidan growls, his tail vibrating in anticipation of a fight. He's looking around, trying to see everywhere at once. That sound has to be coming from somewhere, but where?

We wait until it sounds again. This time I'm ready and don't jump, but I decide on a direction and head for it. Shidan rushes forward until he's a step ahead, which is fine with me. I'm not going to be a hero when I have a perfectly capable man to take that role.

I put my hand on his back for reassurance more than anything as we move slowly closer to the source of the sound. My stomach ties itself into knots over and over as sweat beads on my back. We're moving towards what looks like another set of doors, but these are shiny. So shiny that I can see us approaching them.

We're close enough now I see a pad next to the doors. Shidan walks up to them and the screech sounds again. He roars and smashes the pad before I can stop him. His fist had made short work of the material that it was made of. Wires and pieces of what look like plastic dangle from the newly made hole in the wall.

"Damn it, Shidan," I say, "that might have been—"

I cut off my own words as the doors slide open to reveal an empty box. An elevator, or for all the world what looks like one.

"Well…" I say instead, trailing off.

Shidan walks in and looks it all over carefully. He studies the ceiling then shakes his head. I step in with him. The ceiling is clear, allowing me to see an empty tunnel that rises straight up. I don't see any lifts, cables, or other mechanics that I expect though. How does this lift work?

Next to the doors is another pad. Shidan eyes it sidelong, so I step between him and it.

"Uh-uh," I say shaking my finger at him. "No. We're not going to test our luck yet again."

I study the pad, but it reveals nothing. I touch it and it lights up with a soft greenish glow. The doors screech, try to close, jerk, then the original screech we heard sounds and the entire box shudders so hard I lose my balance. I fall into Shidan who catches me, then the force of gravity slams down on us.

"Oh!" I exclaim as I'm dropped to my ass.

The elevator is racing up, fast. Too damn fast. My stomach is left way below, thankfully. If it was here, I think I'd be sick. Shidan is hunched protectively over me, but when I look around him, I see we're rocketing up.

As fast as it started, it stops with a hard shake and a shudder. The doors screech and open, letting us out into a new room.

This room is much smaller, than the one we left, like an office space or a welcome room or something. Almost a foyer, and there's a ladder on the opposite side from us. Shidan and I hold hands as we walk across the barren space, and he grabs hold of the ladder. He slides the packs off his back and then jerks on it. Satisfied with its solidity, he climbs up. It's not far to the ceiling and I can see from here that there's a hatch.

He works himself up on the ladder until his shoulder is on the hatch and he's crouched on the ladder. He grunts and heaves. Sand pours in around him as he continues to strain, then the hatch flips open, and the welcome red suns beams through the opening. He sticks his head out and looks around, then climbs out.

I start up the ladder but stop partway, waiting for an all clear. In a few moments, his head pops over the edge, and he reaches a hand down, helping me up and out. We're in the open! I take a deep, cleansing breath. I never would have thought I'd be so grateful to see the sand stretching out all around me as far as I can see, but here we are.

Shidan climbs back into the hole, and a few moments later I help tug the packs up and out. Once he's back out, we shut the hatch, and he shoulders the packs. He nods and we start walking. I'm lost, but he seems to know the way.

We don't go far before I can see the glimmer of the dome and know we're on the right track. When we climb the last dune before the City, I look at him and grin.

"Race you!" I say, taking off before I finish the sentence.

I run down the hill laughing. Shidan comes behind me. I can hear the pack shifting as it works to slow him down. I glance back over my shoulder and miss my next step. Before I can stop myself, I'm tumbling head over heels down the dune.

When I come to a stop at last, sand is in every crack and crevice, but I can't stop laughing. The look of concern on Shidan's face only makes me laugh harder. He lands lightly in front of me having leaped down over half the dune. He kneels down, grabbing my shoulder, and staring intently into my face.

"I'm fine," I say, still laughing. "I hate to say it, but that was fun!"

His brow furrows as he frowns. I climb to my feet with his help, then gather up the packs I was carrying, since they scattered up and down the dune as I fell. Shidan helps and we're done much faster than I could have done. I kiss him, letting my fingertip linger. The answer has to be here with us. I can't lose him.

Now it's time to find out. Together we head for Addison.

"This is great," Addison says.

She looks even worse than when we left. Her cheeks and eyes are sunken, making it clear she hasn't slept much, if any at all, since we left.

"Nothing was labeled so we brought all we could," I say.

I've already told her about everything we saw in there, and now I'll need to debrief with Rosalind too. Shidan shifts his weight back and forth and keeps looking around. The way his tail twitches and his wings twitch are all signs he's nervous or uncomfortable. It isn't until he starts pacing that I really begin to worry though.

"Shidan?" I ask, stepping into his path.

Shidan glares, mouth moving, struggling to say something. I wait, patient. I can't imagine what he's going through or how this is affecting him.

"Mal-co-lm," he growls.

"Malcolm?" I ask and he nods. "What about him?"

His face contorts with anger.

"Whe-re?" he asks.

"He's with Jolie, you know this," I say, worrying. "We'll go see him soon."

"Everything okay?" Addison asks.

Shidan growls, baring his teeth. It's actually frightening. I take a step back, and then everything goes wrong. Ladon or Ormarr slam against their door hard enough that the sound echoes through the room, and at the same time Melchior enters the room.

Shidan moves like lightning. My mind doesn't register what's happening until it's happened. Shidan hits Melchior, whose arms are loaded with stuff. Melchior is knocked into the wall, items flying around, as Shidan runs past him.

"SHIDAN!" I yell.

"Stop him!" Addison yells.

Melchior pushes off the wall and gives chase. I'm behind him, unable to keep up with his much longer legs. Melchior skids around a corner, and something hits him, hard. He stumbles to the side, hits the wall, then roars in rage and pain. There's blood running from his forehead.

He pushes off the wall, staggers, and Shidan flies into him, roaring. He's lost to the bijass, more animal than man. His fists slam into Melchior before Melchior can get his bearings, hitting him over and over until Melchior drops.

Shidan stops, looks at me with wild, bloodshot eyes and growls. I stumble back, heart pounding, stomach fluttering. He's lost, but when we lock eyes, something happens. I can't say what exactly, but his face shifts, and almost he looks like he's in control.

Melchior rises behind Shidan. I need to keep him distracted. My chest clenches until it feels like my heart can't beat. I take a step toward him. My own instincts screaming not to approach, feeling the danger, the predator he is.

"Shidan," I say, my voice quavering. "Plea—"

Before I finish the word, Melchior acts. He grabs Shidan, hooking an arm around his neck and jerking back and up. Shidan is lifted off his feet. He fights, wildly. Legs kicking, tail swinging, he slams his elbows backwards, but Melchior has shifted around and is holding him on his side, keeping Shidan from being able to make contact.

Tears run down my face from seeing him fight, seeing him hurt, but what choice do I have?

"I'm sorry," I wail. "So sorry, Shidan!"

He stops trying to hit Melchior with his elbows, both his hands grabbing the arm around his neck choking him. Melchior pulls harder as Shidan struggles less and less until his arms drop and he hangs limp. Melchior holds him longer still.

"Let him go!" I cry out. "You're going to hurt him!"

Melchior doesn't listen. He keeps his tight grip on around Shidan's throat. I run and hit him, pounding my fists on his arm and chest. It bruises my fists, and they throb with pain, but it does nothing to affect Melchior.

He finally loosens his grip, and Shidan slides to the floor unconscious. I drop next to him, sobbing. I lift his head into my lap, and my tears fall onto his beautiful face. Addison's feet appear in one corner of my blurry vision. I can't stop sobbing.

I've lost him. I've lost my love. All that we've built is gone, and I don't think there's going to be a way back. This is it. I'm alone.

Addison crouches down and wraps an arm around my shoulders, pulling my head onto her shoulder. I can't speak. Words are useless anyway. There are no words that are going to bring him back.

"We need to lock him up," Addison says. "Before he wakes up. We can't let him be free."

"No," I sob, though I know it is the right thing. I know it has to happen, but I can't. I can't let him go. If we lock him up, it's over.

Melchior grabs Shidan's arms and tugs him off my lap. I leap to my feet and slap his face. My hand stings, then throbs. Melchior doesn't say a word as he lifts Shidan and places him over his shoulders.

"NO!" I scream. "No, no, no, no, no!"

I drop to my knees as hope dies. I've failed. Addison holds me again and we sit in the hall while I sob, my heart breaking. Melchior walks towards the lab. I can't leave him. If this has to happen, I need to be the one who locks him away. I need him to see me, for him to have some hope. Whatever small glimmer of it I can give him, I must. Rising, I wipe my face with the heels of my hands and walk after Melchior.

"Careful!" I yell as Shidan's head cracks against the door Melchior is trying to get through.

Melchior glances back, blood caking his left eye closed, but he nods. Addison moves past me and holds the door open so that Melchior can get through it easier. We make our way through the lab and into the hall where they've been locking the others up. The hall we enter seems longer. A death march is what it feels like as we walk down it.

There's an empty room, past both Ladon and Ormarr. I jump when Ladon slams against the door, roaring. Ormarr glares out the window of his, teeth bared. It's not only scary, it kills the last glimmers of hope that I'm desperately clinging to.

Addison opens the door to what is going to be Shidan's cell. The open door yawns onto a dim room with thick, reinforced walls. Melchior turns sideways and slides into the opening. He's being careful to at least try not to hurt Shidan.

Suddenly Shidan growls and his tail sweeps around, slamming against the back of Melchior's legs. Melchior drops to the ground and Shidan slams his knee into Melchior's head.

CRACK!

Bile rises in my throat at the sound. "Shidan! NO!"

Addison races into the fray. Shidan grabs her by the front of her shirt lifting her off her feet. He pulls her close to his face and growls. Addison blanches, lips trembling, and her body shaking. I run in too, grabbing his face with both my hands. I tug him around to me.

His eyes are bloodshot, his lips curled back, his tail is sticking up behind his head. He looks from me to the room behind him. His growl is low, deep, rumbling in my core.

"Shidan, no," I beg him, voice quavering. "It's for you."

"Son," he growls and tosses Addison aside.

She hits the wall with a thud and a cry of pain, sliding down. I shake my head, put my hands on his chest, try with all I have to shove him into the doorway. I know it's the right thing to do. He needs to calm down, time to fight this disease. Time for Addison to find a cure. If only a little time, it's all we need.

He bends his knees, dropping lower so his face is level with mine. He stares into my eyes, and a rumble emerges from his lips. He shakes his head.

"You?" he asks, and the disappointment in his eyes is clear.

He steps around me, effortlessly. He doesn't harm me, doesn't lay a hand on me, but he moves past leaving me behind.

"Shidan, no! Please!"

He looks over his shoulder. His eyes narrow, his jaw tenses, but the beast rolls off of him. It washes across my skin, making it clear the man I know and love isn't in control. The animal is.

He bursts into a run and disappears. In shock, I stand there shaking. My knees are too weak to stay standing, so I drop to the floor. The sharp pain brings focus. He's gone.

"Melchior!" Addison yells behind me.

I can't sit here doing nothing. Climbing to my feet I turn to see if she's okay. She kneels beside Melchior. There's blood pooled on the floor around his head. She tears part of her shirt off and dabs at the wound on his head. He stirs, eyes opening, then he roars. Melchior leaps to his feet.

"Where is he?" Melchior growls.

"I don't know," I say, my thoughts a confused mess. "He asked about— oh shit..." My mouth is dry, throat clenched tight as I shake. "Malcolm."

15

AMARA

*M*elchior is faster than I am, outpacing me until he's a blur in the distance, at least a city block ahead of me. The stitch in my side burns, and I can't catch a deep enough breath, but I keep running. Feet pounding the pavement as hard and as fast as I can move.

The look on his face when he looked at me is seared into my thoughts. I can't shake it, can't quit looking at it. Even as I run, it's overlaid on the world around me. I hurt him. He thinks I betrayed him.

Shidan is after our son. The worst part is, I understand it. He's regressing, and what's the one choice no parent wants to ever make? Your child or your love. I know what choice I would make, and it's clear Shidan has done the same.

That primal need to protect, to be dominant, has taken over. I have to get to Jolie before Shidan does. He might hurt her, or Sverre, or… god knows what. Faster! Run faster! Stupid, stupid, stupid. I should have seen this coming. All the little signs I ignored are now flashing neon signs in my head.

Attacking Melchior. The way he was pacing. The little

looks. All signs. All ones I missed. I should have known where his thoughts were going.

Life may be a series of moments, but that makes this the worst moment of mine. I've lost both my guys. The empty streets echo my footsteps back, mocking. It sounds like an admonishment with each motion forward. *Idiot, idiot, idiot.*

We shouldn't have tried to lock him up. I could have reasoned with him. Made him understand before we locked him away. It was only for a little bit, Addison is going to find a cure. She has to.

I'm almost there. It's hard to see, everything is blurry, sweat stings my eyes, and my heart is pounding. I race up the broken stairway to Jolie's, but as soon as I hit the hallway my stomach knots and time stops.

The door to her apartment hangs ajar.

Shit.

"JOLIE!" I yell, a burst of adrenaline washing away the pains.

I burst through her door and enter a nightmare. Jolie is huddled in a corner, curled around Rverre. She's white as a ghost when she looks up, tears streaking down her face. Melchior looms large over her, and there is no sign of Sverre.

"I'm sorry," she says, shaking. "I'm so sorry."

The light creeps slowly across the wall. I know, analytically, that it's marking the passage of time, but time doesn't matter. The emptiness in my heart and soul will never heal. There isn't enough time in the universe for that.

I screwed up. I don't know what I could have done different, despite the fact I've replayed every moment over and over at least a million times. I keep looking for that one instance, that moment that if I had done something different, this wouldn't be happening.

Shidan is out of the City. I don't know where, but I know he has our son. Normally I'd never think twice about Shidan having our son, but he's regressed. He's more animal than he is man thanks to this blasted disease.

I should be out there hunting them, but how? The quarantine is still in effect. We can't get close to each other, and we sure as heck can't have the Zmaj group up. If they did, we could lose them all. So what do I do? Despair is a black maw yawning and eating all my thoughts.

"I'm going to get him," I say, leaping to my feet.

"Amara," Jolie says. "You can't."

"Like hell I can't!" I yell. "I'm the only one who can. He'll listen to me. My man is still in there. He's still Shidan, only more primal, it doesn't take away the basic man."

"Sure," Jolie agrees. "You're right as far as you go. How are you going to make it across the desert? How are you going to track him? How are you going to handle running into a herd of bivo? A flight of sismis? A pack of guster? Or god—"

"Melchior can come with us," I say.

"And how long before he loses it?" Jolie asks. "He's been exposed. If he doesn't lose it, then Addison will need him, because that would mean he's immune. He could be the key to a cure in that case."

"Sverre?" I ask, grasping at straws.

She doesn't have to speak, the look on her face says it all. It's the same situation. We can't risk Sverre either, and he's showing signs too. We can't risk any of them. Jolie walks over and places her hands on my arms, squeezing.

"You know he can't go either," she says softly.

"Enough! I get it!" I yell, throwing my hands up in the air.

I want to punch something. Throw something. Anything but

stay here in this damned apartment waiting for... what? I can't answer that. Addison is working on a cure, but what if she doesn't find one? What if she does, but it's too late? There are too many what-ifs clogging my thoughts. No answers, only more worries.

"I get it," Jolie says softly.

I'm sure she does, especially with Sverre showing signs of the illness too. Despite all our precautions, it is still spreading. Sverre locked himself away before risking exposing his daughter, or so we all hope.

"I have to find him," I say. "I can't just sit here and do nothing."

"Right," Jolie sighs. "Okay, how do we do this?"

I look at her sidelong. "How do we do what?"

"Go out there and get him," she says determinedly. "We're not incapable. If we plan it, take every precaution possible, we can do this."

My jaw falls open, but she's serious. That determined gleam in her eye is all the sign I need. Jolie has always been a bit crazy, but this is beyond the pale. And I like it.

"We need supplies," I say. "And weapons. Are any of those shock sticks that we had working?"

"I think Bert has a couple stashed away that still have a charge," Jolie says.

"What about guns?" I ask.

"No, the guns all died a long time ago," she says. "We've got nothing that works."

"I see the people on guard duty with them all the time," I say.

"For show only. They don't fire," she says.

"Crap," I say.

"Yeah," she says. "But... we can bring Calista."

"Calista? Why?" I ask.

"One, it will be good for her. She's going crazy too, unable to help Ladon, so give her something to do. Two, she's smart. Three, well, power in numbers."

"So you want the first three girls to mate with Zmaj, to go into the desert alone?"

"I do," she says, hands on her hip.

Jolie is tiny. So small she makes me feel big, and I'm not a big girl either, but the defiance beaming on her face is challenging me, daring me to stand against her. It's one of the things I've always admired about her. She may be tiny, but she's fierce.

"We'll be like the three musketeers," I say.

"As long as we're not the 'red shirts' that's fine," Jolie says, shaking her head. "This is stupid. Really, really stupid but you're right. We can't just do nothing. Rosalind is going to have a cow."

She's right. Rosalind will never sign off on this venture. If I do this, I'm disobeying a direct order. My thoughts lock up, muscles tense, I can't move, can barely breathe. She won't sign off but if I don't do this... I'm losing him. I can't. I can't lose my man.

"We don't tell her," I say, barely believing the words are mine as I say them

Jolie's eyes wide and her mouth drops open. "Can we... do that?"

"I'm a big girl, I can do whatever in the hell I want," I say defiantly backing up my decision with bravado. It's always gotten me through every other stupid decision I've made.

"But, Rosalind," she says.

"And?" I ask.

Jolie shakes her head silently pursing her lips. Finally she nods. "Okay, we don't tell her."

"Good," I say. "Let's do this."

Jolie goes to leave Rverre with Inga and to convince Bert to let her have the shock sticks. She has a better relationship with him than I do. I'm fairly sure he doesn't like me, and the feeling is mutual. I think he's petty and lets his imagined power go to his head, which rubs me the wrong way.

I go to Calista. She'll be an easy sell. I hope anyway. Sometimes she's too damn much the scientist, but in this case, I think her emotions will rule.

Swallowing hard, I knock on her door and wait. I hear her shuffling around inside, then the door opens a crack and she peeks out.

"Calista," I say. "I need your help."

"Go away," she says.

"No," I say. "I'm not going until you and I talk."

"What's the point?" she asks.

It's easy to see her eyes are bloodshot and puffy. The bit of her face I can see is gaunt and pale. She hasn't been eating either.

"Open the door," I say.

"No," she says and pushes it closed.

I thrust my foot into the opening before it can latch. The one eye I can see widens and her face flushes, giving her more the appearance of the Calista I know.

"I said, open the damn door," I push against it, but she leans on it, so I don't get it open very far.

"I don't need your attitude," Calista snaps. "You've always been such a bitch. Why can't you leave me alone?"

"Because this bitch knows you need me," I snap, cheeks warming at her insult. "And I need you."

The last is hard to admit after the insult, but that's what does the trick. She stares, eyes narrowing, then she opens the door.

"What is it?" she asks, walking away without bothering to invite me in.

I take a deep breath and try to steady myself, so that when I say it, I won't bust out bawling, again.

"Shidan, he... he..." I clench my fists, squeeze my eyes shut, and force the words out. "He took Malcolm."

"He what?"

"Took him," I say, keeping my eyes squeezed tight. Malcolm's sweet face passes across the blackness of my closed eyelids.

"Where'd they go?" Calista asks.

"He made it out of the City," I say, opening my eyes at last.

Calista stands with her back to me, one hand resting on the counter. Her shoulders are slumped, her clothes wrinkled and stained, and she's definitely lost weight. Even her hair is hanging limp.

"He's got it?" she asks, not looking up or at me.

"Yeah," I say, knowing exactly what it she is referring to.

Calista nods, then rubs her face. "Let me clean up."

And like that, I have her. She's with us. I can see the wisdom of Jolie's plan. Calista needs something to be doing, too. The waiting is killing her, like it would me if I did it, but I'm not going to.

It doesn't take her long before she's washed her face and dressed. As she ties her hair back into a bun, there's a knock at the door. I answer for her, and Jolie is there.

"Got them," she says, holding up the shock sticks. "And a bit more too."

She hands the sticks to me and then slips off her backpack. She opens it to show the contents which is brimming with foodstuffs and the basic things we'll need to survive outside the dome for a few days at least.

"How'd you get him to give up all this?" I ask.

Jolie shrugs. "Bert likes me."

"Must be nice," I say.

Jolie smiles, but it's easy to see she's biting off what she wants to say.

"Say it," I say.

"You could be nicer," she says, diplomatically.

"He could be less of a jerk!" I snap.

"Exactly," Jolie says, nodding.

I'm not an idiot, and I get the point, but it does nothing to lessen my irritation at it. Whatever, we have what we need. Bert can be a jerk as much as he wants. I don't care.

"Let's go," Calista says. "How much of a head start does he have?"

"Half a day," I say.

"This is going to be hard," she says. "His trail will be mostly obscured by now. Any idea where he might head?"

I frown, thinking it over. "He had a cave that he took me to once. He said it was where he lived before he saw our ship crashing."

"Good, it's a starting point," Calista says. "How far?"

I hesitate before saying it, not wanting it to be what it is.

"Four days, maybe five," I say.

Jolie whistles and shakes her head.

"You know the direction?" Calista asks.

"Yes," I say. We stare at each other, and I have one question that won't go away. One thing I don't want to say, I don't want to look at, but there is no choice. "What do we do... when we find him?"

Defiance and fire flash in Calista's eyes. "You reach your man and bring him home."

My heart leaps into my throat and tears fill my eyes. I nod, lip trembling, so I bite it. The pain forces me to focus. Barring a cure there's no other choice. Jolie puts a hand on the small of my back. A reassuring touch.

"Right," I choke out.

"Good," Calista says. "We need to move. He's going to be faster than we are. Traveling with Malcolm might slow him down. That's our best chance to catch up."

We quickly divide up the supplies between us, and in almost

no time we're heading out of the City. As we emerge into the heat from under the dome, I can see his fading tracks heading across the sand. My stomach drops seeing how faded they already are. Tracking him is not going to be possible by his trail for long.

"We're going on your memory," Calista says. "Is that the direction you remember?"

Closing my eyes I call up the memory of that trip. It's been a long time, and it doesn't help that there aren't a lot of markers to navigate by on Tajss. As far as I can tell though, it seems right, so I nod.

"Yeah."

"Okay, then we should move," Calista says.

And we do. Hours pass. The suns move across the sky and drop towards the horizon. The trail has been gone for a long time, and we're not completely dependent on my old memories of a trip I made once.

I'm exhausted, emotionally and physically drained. Every step burns, but it's not only in my muscles. My nerves are fried. Walking, head down, it's almost easier to believe this is some kind of nightmare. That if I keep on moving, sooner or later I'll wake up, and it will all have been a bad dream.

I'm so lost in the blackness of my own thoughts, I bump into Calista. Only then do I look up and out of my own head. We're standing on top of a pretty high dune. I can see for miles around us, out to the last rays of the suns clawing at the horizon as if they don't want to set.

"What's happening?" I ask.

"If we stop for the night, we'll never catch him," Calista says.

"But we can't track him in the dark," Jolie says.

"No," Calista agrees. "But we're not tracking him anyway. We're going off Amara's memory. If we keep moving, we have the best chance of catching him."

I take a deep breath and close my eyes. I need a moment.

I'm doing my darndest to not give in to despair, and it's hard. Everything seems to be working against me. My legs hurt so bad I want to cut them off to make it stop, my lower back is a throbbing knot of pain, and I've got a pressure headache from unshed tears to top it off.

"Right," I say. "We should keep going."

"Can you tell the way?" Calista asks. "We don't want to miss a sign in the dark."

"I'm more worried about the sismis deciding we're dinner," I say.

"It's a definite possibility," Calista says. "But if we don't do this, our only hope will be to make it all the way to the cave he showed you. That's a long ways to travel."

"The longer we're out here, the greater the odds of running into something we don't want to meet with," Jolie adds. "I agree, we should keep moving."

I nod, too exhausted to speak. Jolie slips her pack off and kneels beside it. She digs through and pulls out some chunks of smoked guster that she hands to each of us. I pop the piece right into my mouth. It's tough and chewy, but it does have an invigorating effect.

Calista passes around the waterskin, and I pull out some carefully wrapped epis from my pocket. We each take a piece, then we shoulder our packs and continue our journey. The nightmare journey from hell.

The quest to save my son and my husband. If I can.

The dark on Tajss isn't like dark on the ship. 'Night' on the ship was manufactured. A timer that dimmed the lighting so it would coincide with the normal cycle of a day. The entire point was to keep us used to being on a planet. Only it didn't fully succeed, at least not for Tajss.

On the ship, night was never like this. Sometimes the suns on Tajss set before the moons rise, and for an hour or more, there is this pitch-black darkness that has to be experienced to be believed. It's the most dangerous time on the planet because you really can't see anything. Even the Zmaj have a hard time seeing, it's so dark.

Problem is that a lot of the predators that want to make a tasty meal out of us, don't have the same problem. There are some that have adapted to make this their best hunting time. They don't hunt by sight but by sound. Sound, like the shuffling of our feet as we fight our way through the sand.

The sand on Tajss is constantly blowing, so it's loose. Every step you sink in, and it's a guess—will it be to your ankle? Mid-calf? Up to your knee? The Zmaj use their wings and tails to move their heavier bodies across the sand as if it's nothing. Us humans aren't designed for this. All of which means, we're noisy.

Really noisy.

Which, of course, is bad. I know of three major predators on the planet. The sismis that fly in groups. They're big, each one the size of a Zmaj at least, so around seven feet across with leathery wings. They only come out at night, which is why conventional wisdom is not to travel in the dark.

Then there are the guster, which are massive predatorial lizards. They move around on hind legs and have enough razor-sharp teeth to tear apart anything that moves. Worse, they hunt in packs, making them incredibly dangerous.

Neither of them compare to the zemlja. Zemlja give me nightmares. Huge worm-like creatures that burrow through the ground, hunting. They leave massive tunnels in their wake and hunt completely by sound. The slightest noise can attract one. I've seen them too many times, and even the best Zmaj fighters fear tangling with one of them. They can be as big as a building and I've heard talk of them getting even bigger.

Calista and Jolie, botanists by trade, have talked about how without the zemlja there wouldn't be epis. Epis grows in the caverns they leave behind in their passage. The zemlja excrete their waste as they travel, and in that waste the epis grows.

Epis extends life, and god knows what else. It's addictive, but absolutely vital for humans to survive on this planet. It changes your DNA, adjusting it so we can stand the heat and not die. Unless we quit taking it, of course. Then you go into withdrawals and die.

So, noise on Tajss is bad, and humans struggling to travel across the desert are noisy. Traveling at night adds in even more layers of danger. And yet, here we go. Calista and Jolie didn't hesitate to help me. They both have every reason in the world not to do this. Kids at home, their mates are back there, but they're with me.

Tears swell in my eyes as I think about it while forcing one foot in front of the other. I don't deserve friends like this. I've never been nice and I know it. Most everyone thinks I'm a bitch, probably because I am. I've got all my excuses: rough life, being the only female pilot, and outcast. But that's it, isn't it? They're excuses. Reasons that sound good, and I can use them like I do, as armor.

Armor that protects me. The truth is, I've been scared my entire life. Scared of being rejected. Scared of being alone. In this stupid, terrible moment, it hits me. I'm not alone. Despite the fact that I've been an insufferable jerk to both of these women, they're here with me. Without question, they threw in with me, and they're putting their very lives on the line.

"Guys," I huff.

I can barely tell that Calista and Jolie both look, but they don't stop or speak. I swallow, trying to force moisture back into my mouth. The dark is helping. They're dim outlines, barely real people, it's almost as if I'm on my own, talking to myself.

"I want to... thank you," I say. "I know I'm not, I've never been, uh, I'm not a nice person. I never have been."

Calista snorts.

"Amara, it's fine," Jolie says consolingly.

"No, it's not," I say. "It's really not. I don't deserve friends like you. I'm not sure I deserve a man like Shidan, and Malcolm…"

I trail off, my throat clenching tight as I think about my son. One of them pats my arm. I'm more grateful than ever for the darkness hiding the tears streaming down my face.

"You'd do the same for us," Calista says.

"I would," I choke out. "I really, really would. I'm going to be better. Somehow, I'll change. If only we can… find my… son."

I'm sobbing and can't say any more. I'm shouting my prayers in my head. Begging God, the universe, anyone or anything that will listen. Let my son be okay. Please don't take him from me. I need him. I need them both. I can't go on without either of them.

"We'll find them," Calista says, her voice sounds absolutely certain.

It bolsters my flagging hope. We will find them. We have to. I can't even consider the alternative.

Silence falls over our small group again as we all focus on moving forward. The moons rise. Three of them are showing tonight, casting the world in a silvery light. It's as if the world is turned to black and white. It's beautiful, empty, and cold, but beautiful.

We pause for water, and I turn around in a circle, trying to find any landmark I can use to guide us by, something more than the instinct I'm running on. I'm all for a mother's instincts, but I'd like to have a guidepost to navigate by. Anything.

"Is that a rock formation way out there?" I ask, pointing.

They move up beside me and stare.

"I think so," Jolie says at last.

"Does it look like an old man with a crooked nose?" I ask.

"Sort of," Calista says, uncertainty in her voice.

"Okay, good, I remember that. When we reach that, we go left. That was a bit over halfway," I say.

"If that's halfway, where did you sleep on your journey?" Jolie asks. "This is too far for straight travel. Shidan never would have had you keep going.

"Shit!" I exclaim. "You're right. There was a small crevasse that he made a camp for us in. It was before that landmark... maybe a quarter of the way to the cave?"

Calista smiles, and a burst of energy floods through all of us. It's clear to see in each of their faces.

"We need to move," Jolie says.

Going downhill is always easier. The biggest problem is getting your feet tangled up in the sand, which sounds stupid until it happens to you. Because you sink in differing depths, when you start picking up momentum, it's easy for one foot to sink in further than you expect, and you're already taking the next step. In an instant, you are no longer running but tumbling, often head over heels. Having done this too many times, all of us move with caution.

Once we reach the more-or-less flat ground before starting up the next dune, all of us run. Or the Tajss equivalent of running. The glimmer of hope bolsters my body. It pushes aside the exhaustion, the aches, and the pains. Nothing touches the black emptiness that continues to threaten my thoughts, but it does help to hold even that at bay.

Up the next dune and down the far side. Almost halfway up the next. I take a step, and my foot keeps sinking until my entire leg is swallowed in the loose spot of sand.

"Ah!" I cry as my foot keeps going in, and then I faceplant into the sand.

I rise up on my arms and try to pull free, but I can't get out of the hole. The sand I'm pushing against to pull myself out is also loose, so my hands sink in. Calista and Jolie come over to help, but can't get too close or risk getting stuck themselves.

"Crap," Calista says, sliding her pack off and setting it down.

"We need a rope or something," Jolie says.

"A good bit of rope. Never travel far without a rope," Calista mutters.

"What in the holy hell are you talking about?" I snap. "We never travel with rope."

Calista looks at Jolie and shakes her head. My cheeks flush, seeing full well I'm not in the loop on some private joke.

"Heathens, what can you do?" Jolie asks, smiling.

"I'm stuck here, are you two going to help or not?" I ask.

"I don't know, she hasn't read *Lord of the Rings*, maybe we should leave her," Calista says.

"Lord of the what?" I ask. "I never had time for reading, I was training!"

"And that is probably why you're the way you are," Calista says.

"What do you mean by that?" I ask.

"Grumpy," Calista says. "You're always grumpy. You don't read, let your mind wander, explore new ideas and possibilities."

I close my eyes and count to ten. It's an old technique and while it has never helped me before it has helped Shidan and I'll hold out hope. My patience is beyond thin at this point. They are looking through packs as they tease me, so at least they're trying to get me out.

"I'm not grumpy," I say at last. "I am stuck. I am worried. I am not grumpy."

"Amara, you're a bitch, and you know it," Jolie says.

Calista laughs, but cuts it off quickly.

"Yeah," I agree. "I am and I'm sorry. Can we get me out of here now?"

"This might work," Calista says. She rises to her feet holding two sticks that will be used for firewood at some point. "If we lie flat, we can each have her take hold of one stick and pull."

"Should work, distribute our weight and allow us to pull her free," Jolie agrees.

"Great, let's do this!" I exclaim, struggling again to break free.

They move around so that they're in front of me, then both lie flat on their stomachs. They inch their way forward, belly-crawling across the sand, with arms outstretched, each holding one of the thick sticks. I stretch my fingers until I'm touching the wood, and at last, I get a hold on them.

"Got it!" I exclaim.

"Good, hold tight," Calista says.

I do, gripping the stick with all I've got. The two of them work their way back, slowly until my arms are being pulled at the socket.

"Try to work your way out now," Jolie says.

I pull myself towards them and start to rise up out of the sand, slowly. So slowly. The sand grips me tight, unwilling to give me up, but it's losing the fight an inch at a time. Jolie grimaces, struggling to hold onto the stick, then she loses her grip and the stick flies out of both our hands and lands next to my head with a thunk.

Sand flies into my eyes and mouth, temporarily blinding me. I sputter and blink rapidly. "Ugh."

"Sorry," Jolie says, "I couldn't hold it."

"Fine," I say, spitting out more sand. I toss the stick back towards her. "Try again?"

She grabs the stick and we try again. I'm almost out, only my calves are still stuck below the sand when something screeches overhead.

"Look out!" Calista yells.

I kick my way out the rest of the way and roll to the side without looking. The screech sounds again, and now I hear the whishing sound of large wings. I roll over and over, unsure of where I am in relation to the other women or anything else.

At last I stop and look, immediately wishing I hadn't. A flock of sismis circle and dive not fifty feet away, tracking along with Calista as she keeps rolling.

"KEEP MOVING!" I yell.

The sismis rise into the sky, and then they're diving my way. I leap to my feet, spin away, and run. The back of my neck tingles as the hairs rise in fear, and on instinct, I dive forward and roll. Their leather wings whoosh over so I keep rolling.

"HERE!" Jolie yells.

I stop my roll and get on my hands and knees. Jolie is running in a different direction, buying time. How much time can we buy before one of us slips? Eventually they're going to get their nasty fangs into someone.

Thoughts race past. I need a solution, but I've got nothing. Not even any bad ideas to throw away aside from what we're doing. Maybe they'll get tired of working so hard for their prey? If we don't slip, if nothing goes wrong, no one hits a soft spot in the sand. If, if, if, all possibilities are bad.

Calista yells, pulling them towards her. My stomach is in knots as I climb to my feet and yell attracting their attention back my way. They spin in the air. A black mass of flapping wings and what I know to be very sharp rows of teeth.

I run as fast as I can until I hear them too close when I dive and roll until I hear Jolie yell. We repeat the cycle over and over, but we're getting really spread out. How much further can we go before we can't yell loud enough to pull them off whoever happens to be the unlucky girl?

Closing my eyes, I take a deep breath, then yell. I'm not going to dive this time. I'll keep them on me and hope I can outrun them. I'm not going to put my friends at risk for me. I don't deserve it, and I should be better to them.

Once I see the sismis turn and come my direction, I run. I

need to make it far enough that Calista and Jolie's yells won't be enough to pull them off. I'm sorry Shidan, tell Malcolm how much I love him.

My heart breaks, and tears stream down my face, but this is the right thing to do, and I'm going to go through with it. The screeches ring in my ears. They're closing in. I don't have long until I'll feel their claws and teeth tearing into my flesh.

I hope it doesn't hurt too much.

I can't see where I'm running because of the tears. Everything is blurred by the tears, but I slam into something hard. It roars. A deep, reverberating sound that shakes my guts with its depth. It sounds angry.

"AHHHH!" I scream in terror. I stumble back and trip over my feet before I land on my ass.

A flash of orange, then heat washes over my body. The roar sounds again, and this time the screeching seems different. Afraid almost.

I roll to the side and throw an arm over my face, trying to clear the tears away so I can see what new threat has emerged. When I come to a stop and get onto my hands and knees, my heart leaps into my throat.

"MOMMY!" Malcolm yells, racing across the sand towards me.

"Baby!" I scream, half-rising and running for my baby.

I scoop him up into my arms and curl my body protectively around him. Only then do I see Shidan. Shidan belches fire into a massive ball of flame that explodes in the middle of the swarm of sismis. He swings his lochaber in wide, wild arcs. The sharp blade whistles as it slices through the air. Then it hits a sismis, making a meaty sound followed by a scream of pain, which is cut off when the beast drops to the ground.

Shidan roars, opening his arms and wings wide, calling all the world to him. He belches a fresh bout of flame, the red-orange fire making a ball in the air, singeing the sismis. The cloud of creatures disperses around the fire and then they retreat, moving on in search of easier prey.

Shidan watches from a few feet away. His eyes are blood-shot, his muscles bulging, blood covering his bare chest. I'm frozen in place, unable to move. My heart pounds, blood rushing to my head and I'm light-headed, clinging to Malcolm.

"It's okay, Mommy," Malcolm whispers in my ear.

Malcolm wraps his arms so tight around my neck it's choking me. He kisses my cheek then eases his grip.

"Shidan," I force his name past the lump blocking my throat.

He doesn't answer, chest heaving, he swings the lochaber up. My heart stops, stomach clenching, but he continues the motion and puts it away on his back. Our staring contest resumes. I hear Jolie and Calista approaching, but I'm too scared to even glance at them. I can't take my eyes off him. I'm not sure if he sees me, our son, or if he's a completely wild animal.

No. This is Shidan. He's there, this disease may have made him regress, but he's still him. He's my man, my treasure, and he loves me.

"Go to him," Malcolm encourages.

Hesitantly, I take a step forward. My limbs tremble, and I don't dare breathe. My foot touches down, and I slowly commit my weight to it, never taking my eyes off of his. His eyes dart past me, then back. A tremor moves through his wings, and his tail twitches. I start another step, toes touching down, keeping my weight back, ready to run.

Run where?

"Shidan," I repeat. "It's me. I love you."

Still, he doesn't move. His eyes bore into me, but behind his eyes I see something flash. The corners of his lips twitch. His hands unclench and some of the tension in his body eases out of it. His breathing is still rapid but after the fight that's to be expected.

Another step. I'm within his arms' reach. Malcolm shifts, wrapping his legs around my waist, turning to face his father.

"Daddy!" Malcolm exclaims. "See! I told you Mommy wasn't being mean. It only seemed like it."

"No honey, Mommy wasn't being mean. Mommy only wanted to help, to do the right thing."

Talking eases my nerves as I keep moving closer. Shidan doesn't move, watching, and then I'm so close we could touch. I hesitate. We're inches apart, but I don't touch him. If he's going to do something, if he wants to hurt me for my perceived betrayal, this is going to be it. Craning my neck, I stare up and wait.

He doesn't move, so I reach out with my free hand, keeping Malcolm in place with the other.

His scales are cool to the chest. I want, with all my heart, to lay my head on his chest and feel him wrap his arms around me. I want him to hold me, tell me I'm forgiven, that everything is okay. He doesn't move, except to drop his eyes to where my hand rests on his chest.

"Shidan, please," I whisper. "Please come back to us."

I can't tell what's happening with him. His eyes are so bloodshot, they're almost all red. He doesn't blink, doesn't move. I know, though, that he sees me. His brow furrows, then his mouth moves.

"Tre-as-ure," he says, struggling to form the word.

"Yes!" I exclaim, heart leaping into my throat.

Tears streaming, I choke and raise my hand from his chest to his face. He leans forward. It's only a slight motion, but it's the first positive movement he's made.

I hear Calista and Jolie coming up. Shidan straightens and growls. He wraps his arm around me and jerks me to his side. I'm so surprised, I almost drop Malcolm. Shidan glares at the women, and there's a deep rumble in his chest.

"Stay back!" I yell.

They stop, both of them holding their hands up, palms facing us.

"Stay cool, Shidan, we're here to help," Calista says.

He doesn't answer with words, but he does growl and takes a step backwards.

"Okay, big guy," Calista says, making a patting motion with her hands.

Terror swells in my guts. I can't let him steal me away too. That would defeat the entire point of coming out here. It's clear that's where this is heading. I have to put a stop to this entire mess, right now. I have to reach him, get him to fight his way out of the grips of his bijass.

After jerking myself free of his grip, I step around and in front of him. I raise my free hand and point my finger at him.

"That's enough!" I yell. "Shidan, you come back to me right now. You're not weak, you can fight this, and you damn well better!"

His eyes widen, his mouth drops open, but he stops growling. It's all the encouragement I need to keep going.

"I've had enough. You've scared me, you are scaring me right now, and worse, you're scaring Malcolm!"

"I'm not scared," Malcolm says.

"Hush," I snap. "Shidan, you listening to me?"

I move in closer, and he takes a step back. He shakes his head from side to side, his frown deepening.

"Come on now, fight this! You can do it!"

He grabs his head with both hands and roars, bending over then dropping to his knees. I stand over him waiting, almost daring to hope. When he looks up the intelligence is in his eyes, but there is something more written on his face. Fear.

He shudders, shakes his head again, then his mouth opens, but no sound comes out. He clenches his jaw, rubs his head, and tries again.

"Am-ara," he says.

"Yes, love, it's me," I say.

He looks from me to Malcolm, then back again. He shakes his head. "Hard. Bijass."

"I know love, I know," I say, tears pouring down my face. "Come home. Please. Addison is going to find a cure. Come back."

"Home," he says, but he looks over his shoulder in the direction he was going.

"NO!" I yell, and he jerks his attention back. "That's not home. Home in the City, with me, with Malcolm. Come home, Shidan."

"Home?" he asks.

He's fighting it. I can see the struggle on his face to hold onto himself.

"Yes," I say, reaching my hand out towards him.

My hand hangs in the empty space between us, waiting. Hoping. I pray. I pray to anyone and everything. I need him. I need him more than air. I can't live without him by my side. I can't do this.

He places his hand in mine and squeezes. I sigh heavily then throw myself into his arms.

"Only Amara could win her man back by being a bitch," Calista whispers behind me.

I don't care. I am who I am, and while I'll strive to be a better person, none of that matters, because Shidan loves me as I am.

16

AMARA

"Will it work?" I ask, biting my lip.

Addison looks up, and her eyes are sunken, bruised from the lack of sleep. Her skin is sallow and it's obvious she's doing all she can to keep it together.

"Yes," she nods. "Or no."

"Or no?" I ask.

"I don't know," she says. "That's the accurate answer. I think so. It looks like it will. It's not like I have a full laboratory. I can't do animal testing and see the results. All I can do is insert this cure into this sample of what I think is the problem. It looks promising."

"So . . . now what?" I ask, biting off all the snarky comments that pop into my head.

I'm trying to be a better person. I am a better person. She's exhausted and has worked tirelessly to find a cure.

"Now we test it," she says, rubbing her eyes. "And then we hope."

"Who's first?" I ask.

"Ladon," she says. "If it works on him, then we'll know it

will work on the others. He's been sick the longest, and he was patient zero."

"Can I help?"

Addison stares at the table, not looking up. "Yeah."

"What's wrong?" I ask.

"We have to give it to him," she says.

"Yeah?" I ask.

"I don't know how we're going to do it," she admits. "He's crazed. Completely primal."

"Calista can do it," I say.

"It's too dangerous," Addison says. "I'd have three of the men come in to hold him but I can't expose them."

"Do Shidan, then," I say. "I was able to reach him once, let's try him first."

Addison doesn't speak for a long time. Then she looks up and nods. The decision made, she prepares a syringe, and then the two of us enter the holding area.

Ladon slams against the door, pounding on it and roaring. It makes me jump every time, even knowing it's coming. I rush past him towards the end of the hall and the room that holds Shidan. I look in the door to his cell, which is what it really is, and squint my eyes to see him.

The cell is dark, and he's at the back of it, crouched down. I can see his outline more than actually see him. It breaks my heart seeing him in there.

"Let me go in alone," I say.

"You need to inject this into his arm," Addison says. "Or butt. Either, or."

"Okay," I say, taking the syringe from her.

She unlocks the door and pulls it open. I walk in and she locks it behind me.

"Shidan," I say. "It's me."

He growls and rises to his feet. My stomach clenches, but I

force myself to take the next step forward. It's small so that one step puts me right at him.

"I've got medicine," I say. "This is going to sting."

A low rumble is his answer, but he doesn't move away. Rising onto my toes I kiss him, running my hands up to his neck, across his shoulders and then down onto his biceps. While he's distracted, I open one eye and then stab him with the syringe.

He jerks back, eyes wide, and growls. I jerk the needle out and step back.

"I'm sorry love," I say. "It will help. It has to help."

He growls, and his eyes look more bloodshot. Then he starts trembling. My heart is racing as the trembling becomes violent, and he drops to the floor.

"ADDISON!" I scream.

The door swings open behind me and she rushes in, answering my call.

"Grab his head!" Addison yells.

I jump to do what she says, grabbing onto his head. He's shaking so much I can barely hold onto it. I keep losing my grip. As I struggle with his head, she forces a thick stick into his mouth.

"What are you doing?" I cry.

"Keeping him from choking on his tongue," she says.

"Oh god, what have I done?" I ask, tears streaming down my face.

"It's fine," Addison says through gritted teeth, struggling to keep Shidan from flailing.

"This is fine?" I yell.

"I expected as much, yes," Addison says. "It will pass. In a minute."

"You expected this!" I exclaim. "Why didn't you warn me?"

"In… a… minute…"

The convulsions begin to ease, becoming less violent, and it becomes less of a struggle to hold him down. At last he lies peacefully, almost as if he's sleeping. My tears drip onto his sweet face.

"Is he..." I can't finish the thought.

Addison rises to her feet and dusts herself off.

"Yeah," she says. "He'll be fine. Come on, let him rest."

"Can we..." I rise, looking down at him and know the answer to my question.

We can't lift him. He's too big. He'll have to rest here, on the floor. We exit the room and Addison shuts and locks the door behind us. As she walks away, I lean against it, pressing my face to the small window, watching. Hoping. Waiting for him.

17

AMARA

Something touches my cheek. I slap it away, not ready to wake up.

There's another touch, and I force my eyes open. They are heavy and sticky with sleep, but the moment I open them I gasp. Shidan's face is smiling, inches from mine.

"Shidan?"

"Yes, my love," he says.

I leap into his arms, planting a kiss on his face. He wraps his arms around me and stands, lifting me up. I don't want to let him go. I don't want this to be a dream. Every part of my body hurts, but I don't care. I must have fallen asleep next to his door ,and now he's here. He's really here, with me, and he's himself once more.

"Ahem," Addison clears her throat loudly, and at last I break our kiss.

She's standing behind us, smiling, but it's easy to see the exhaustion on her face. Shidan lowers me to my feet, but keeps his arm wrapped around me, holding me close.

"The others?" I ask.

"Recovering," she says. "Mostly."

"Mostly?" I ask.

"Ladon is... not responding as quickly as I'd like," she says.

"Is he..." I trail off not wanting to say the words.

"He'll be fine," Addison says emphatically.

"Okay," I say.

She sighs and shakes her head. "I'm sorry. I'm wiped. He is recovering, but slower. We're keeping him under observation for now. He hasn't regained all his memories, but the aggression has receded."

"That's good, right?" Shidan asks.

"Yes," Addison agrees. "It's much better. Rosalind will want to see you, by the way."

"I'm not surprised," I say. "We should go meet with her."

"I agree," Shidan says.

"I'm going to check on Ladon, then I'm going to catch some sleep. If she needs anything—," Addison says, turning and walking away.

"You scared me," I say to Shidan, once we're alone again.

He spins me around and against him, crushing my body to his. His strong arms wrap around my waist, and he lifts me off my feet, planting a firm, insistent kiss on my lips.

"I am sorry," he says. "I can't tell you... how hard it was." I run my hands through his hair then wrap my arms around his neck and squeeze. "I never forgot you. You are my treasure. My truest love."

"I know," I say, tears falling again. "I know."

Inhaling a deep, shaky breath, I straighten up, and he lets me back down to the floor. I wipe my tears away. There's no call for them any longer. He's back.

"There is... one more thing," I say, biting my lip and staring at the ground.

"Whatever it is, we will be together," he says, holding my arms. I can't look up. Butterflies war in my stomach and I'm trembling. "Amara, treasure, what could it be?"

"I'm pregnant," I blurt out.

Silence. Absolute, total silence then...

"YES!" he screams so loud it echoes off the walls, reverberating.

"You're happy?" I ask.

"Of course I am? How could you think otherwise? We are to have another child? This is wonderful!"

"Everything okay?" Addison asks, poking her head back into the hall.

"Yeah," I say. "He's taking the news well."

Addison smiles. "I told you he would."

Shidan lifts me into his arms, cupping an arm under my butt and cradling me against his chest, carefully not crushing my stomach.

"You are the most amazing, wonderful, beautiful female in the universe," he says.

"That's a pretty big statement," I say, cheeks flushing warm.

"It is truth," he says, peppering my face with kisses. "I love you more with every passing moment."

"I love you," I say a fresh round of tears threatening to fall.

Damn emotions. It's the hormones, I swear. I close my eyes and bask in the warmth of his love.

We've conquered the latest challenge Tajss has thrown at us. There will be more, many, many more, I'm sure, but together we'll face them all. My love, my treasure, the one I can't live without, and now our family is going to grow again.

I'm happy, too. Happier than I ever thought I could be. Thank you, Tajss. Thank you for giving me this second chance to be a better person.

Now I can't wait to see what the future brings for us.

THE END

KEEP IN TOUCH

Did you enjoy Dragon's Isolation? Sign up for my newsletter to be the first to know about new releases!

Http://miranamartinromance.com/newsletter

If you missed it, start at the beginning with Dragon's Baby (Red Planet Dragons of Tajss Book 1).

If you want to know more about how the survivors arrived on Tajss read book one of the Red Planet Jungle series: Red Planet Dragons of Tajss (Red Planet Jungle).

ABOUT THE AUTHOR

USA Today Bestselling Author of fantasy and scifi romance, Miranda Martin's books feature larger than life heroes with out-of-this-world anatomy and smart heroines destined to save the world. As a little girl she would sneak off with her nose in a book, dreaming of magical realms. Today she brings those fantasies to life and adores every fan who chooses to live in them for a while.

She was born and raised in southern Virginia, but as a veteran she's traveled to places like Korea, Hawaii and good 'ole Texas. Now she's settled in Kansas, the heart of America, with her husband and daughters. Her favorite animals are dragons, unicorns and cats. If she's not writing, you can still find her tucked away somewhere with a warm blanket and her nose in a book.

Get in touch!
mirandamartinromance.com
miranda@mirandamartinromance.com

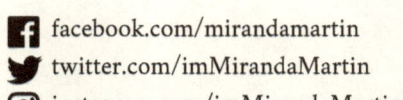

facebook.com/mirandamartin
twitter.com/imMirandaMartin
instagram.com/imMirandaMartin